the iT girl

★ TEAM ★
AWKWARD

★ TEAM ★ AWKWARD

Katy Birchall is the author of
The It Girl. She also works at
Country Life magazine as their
Deputy Features Editor. Katy won
the 24/7 Theatre Festival Award in
2011 for Most Promising New Comedy
Writer with her very serious play
about a ninja monkey at a dinner
party. Her pet Labradors are the loves
of her life, she is mildly obsessed with
Jane Austen and one day she hopes to
wake up as an elf in The Lord of the
Rings. She currently lives in Brixton
with her (apparently) much cooler and
funnier housemate.

Follow her on Twitter @KatyBirchall

and

check out p307 for an exclusive
competition!

KATY BIRCHALL

the iT girl

TEAM AWKWARD

EGMONT

FOR SAM

First published in paperback in Great Britain 2016
by Egmont UK Limited
The Yellow Building, 1 Nicholas Road, London W11 4AN

Text copyright © 2016 Katy Birchall

The moral rights of the author have been asserted

ISBN 978 1 4052 7826 3

www.egmont.co.uk

60876/1

A CIP catalogue record for this title is available from the British Library

Typeset by Avon DataSet Ltd, Bidford on Avon, Warwickshire
Printed and bound in Great Britain by the CPI Group

MIX
Paper
FSC   FSC® C018306

From: jess.delby@zingmail.co.uk
To: anna_huntley@zingmail.co.uk
Subject: You're overreacting

So you got stuck in a plant pot. It's not that big of a deal.

J x

From: anna_huntley@zingmail.co.uk
To: jess.delby@zingmail.co.uk
Subject: Re: You're overreacting

No, you're right. It's not that big of a deal. It's not that big of a deal that a video of me stuck in a plant pot, trying and failing to get out, has been watched on YouTube by MILLIONS OF PEOPLE.

Love, me xxx

From: jess.delby@zingmail.co.uk
To: anna_huntley@zingmail.co.uk
Subject: You're wrong

Excuse you, but you WISH you were that famous. It has not been watched by millions of people, only a few thousand. Let me check and I can tell you the precise -.

WHOA. It's had almost two million views! That's gone up really fast in the last hour.

Do you know what that means? Almost two million people have seen you stuck in a plant pot!

This is the best day of my life.

J x

From: anna_huntley@zingmail.co.uk
To: jess.delby@zingmail.co.uk
Subject: Re: You're wrong

I am never leaving the Hoover cupboard again. I don't care how hard Dad is trying to tempt me out with that plate of duck pancakes he's left right outside the door. I can smell

it. He's even shut Dog in the kitchen so he can't get them.
He thinks he's so clever. HA.

Clearly he does not know me very well if he thinks that
I would be tempted out of hiding by some stupid duck
pancakes.

Honestly, I have more self-respect than that. This is all his
fault in the first place, anyway. If it weren't for him, I wouldn't
be the laughing stock of the ENTIRE country right now.

Love, me xxx

From: jess.delby@zingmail.co.uk
To: anna_huntley@zingmail.co.uk
Subject: What?!

Explain to me how this is your dad's fault?

J x

From: jess.delby@zingmail.co.uk
To: anna_huntley@zingmail.co.uk
Subject: HELLO

Are you there? I sent that last email almost fifteen minutes ago. Why don't you just answer your mobile? You're so useless with your phone.

J x

From: anna_huntley@zingmail.co.uk
To: jess.delby@zingmail.co.uk
Subject: Re: HELLO

Sorry about the delay there, I was just rearranging my cushions. If I'm going to be stuck in here for the rest of my life, this cupboard has to be comfy.

I can't answer my phone because I've turned it off. I've had a crazy amount of calls and texts from people asking me to explain the plant pot situation and the beeping was driving me insane.

Love, me xxx

From: jess.delby@zingmail.co.uk
To: anna_huntley@zingmail.co.uk
Subject: I'm on to you

You went out to get the duck pancakes, didn't you?

J x

From: anna_huntley@zingmail.co.uk
To: jess.delby@zingmail.co.uk
Subject: Re: I'm on to you

Absolutely not. What do you take me for? I am not that weak. Please. Have some faith.

Like I said, I was arranging cushions.

Love, me xxx

From: jess.delby@zingmail.co.uk
To: anna_huntley@zingmail.co.uk
Subject: Stop your lies

Sure. I bet your dad blocked the door with his foot when you reached out to get the duck pancakes, so you were forced to talk to him for a bit. Is that why you took fifteen minutes to reply?

J x

From: anna_huntley@zingmail.co.uk
To: jess.delby@zingmail.co.uk
Subject: Re: Stop your lies

No. I was arranging cushions. Then I replied to your email.

Love, me xxx

From: jess.delby@zingmail.co.uk
To: anna_huntley@zingmail.co.uk
Subject: Re: Stop your lies

I just got this text from your dad:

'Hi Jess, Nick Huntley here. Anna is refusing to come out
of the Hoover cupboard again. Can you try talking to her?
She's eaten the duck pancakes I left out for her. I talked to
her but she tried to slam the door on my foot. N.'

J x

From: anna_huntley@zingmail.co.uk
To: jess.delby@zingmail.co.uk
Subject: Re: Stop your lies

What's your point?

Love, me xxx

From: jess.delby@zingmail.co.uk
To: anna_huntley@zingmail.co.uk
Subject: You're ridiculous

Tell me why you think this is your dad's fault.

J x

From: anna_huntley@zingmail.co.uk
To: jess.delby@zingmail.co.uk
Subject: Re: You're ridiculous

HELLO. Obviously it's his fault.

He's the one who had to have his stupid engagement
celebration party in Helena's stupid house, where she
has stupid palm tree things in her hall sitting in stupidly
massive pots, which innocent victims might stumble
backwards into, get their bottom stuck in and then be
filmed trying to get out on someone's stupid smartphone.

If he had stayed single and not got engaged to the world's most famous actress I would never have got stuck in a palm-tree plant pot and I would be living in PEACE.

And also, why did people FILM it rather than help get me out?! This is what is wrong with the world today. Why did they film it? WHY?!

Love, me xxx

From: jess.delby@zingmail.co.uk
To: anna_huntley@zingmail.co.uk
Subject: Re: You're ridiculous

Because you folded into the pot with your legs sticking up like that and your arms flailing around was really funny.

I've added it to my favourites. And I've bookmarked it. Now I can get it to come up on my screen with just one click.

My dad's watched it five times. He said he's sending it round his entire office first thing in the morning.

J x

From: anna_huntley@zingmail.co.uk
To: jess.delby@zingmail.co.uk
Subject: Re: You're ridiculous

Everyone is going to be laughing at me into the next century. This is the worst way to start the new term.

How come ever since I started there a term ago I've been the official laughing stock of Woodfield?

Love, me xxx

From: jess.delby@zingmail.co.uk
To: anna_huntley@zingmail.co.uk
Cc: dantheman@zingmail.co.uk
Subject: Desperate times

Falling into a palm tree pot is so not the worst way to start a term, Anna. You did that last term. You set Josie Graham on fire, remember?

Look, I've brought Danny into the conversation to cheer you up.

Danny, Anna is upset because she's a YouTube sensation. Any kind words you can throw her way?

J x

From: dantheman@zingmail.co.uk
To: jess.delby@zingmail.co.uk
Cc: anna_huntley@zingmail.co.uk
Subject: Re: Desperate times

I've been looking at the video and it's actually a Dracaena Lisa plant that you fell into, Anna, not a palm tree, although they are often mistakenly identified as palms due to their similar shape. The name Dracaena Lisa comes from the Greek word *drakaina*, which means 'dragon'. This is because, if you cut the stem of the Dracaena, the juice that seeps out resembles dragon's blood.

Danny.

From: anna_huntley@zingmail.co.uk
To: dantheman@zingmail.co.uk
Cc: jess.delby@zingmail.co.uk
Subject: Well, that settles it

I hate my life.

See you guys at school.

Love, me xxx

From: jess.delby@zingmail.co.uk
To: anna_huntley@zingmail.co.uk; dantheman@
zingmail.co.uk
Subject: Re: Well, that settles it

Three million views and counting!

J x

'You know, I think you will find that this whole situation will really boost your popularity,' Jess said, leaning back against the cubicle door.

'How, exactly?'

'For one thing.' She hauled her bag up from the floor sharply, causing her Chemistry book to tumble out on to the bathroom floor. Jess grimaced. 'It makes you . . . approachable.'

'Approachable?!' I pulled my knees closer to my chest, struggling to maintain my balance on top of the closed toilet seat.

'Yes.' Jess shuffled into the corner of the cubicle and awkwardly leaned sideways to pick up her book, her forehead narrowly avoiding my knees. 'Approachable. You're one of the people, just like Princess Diana was.'

'I don't remember Diana, Princess of Wales, ever getting stuck in a plant pot,' I huffed.

'Probably because there were no smartphones back then,' Jess said comfortingly.

'This is so embarrassing.'

Jess looked at me. I could tell that she was less sympathetic than she had been before I'd forced her to cram herself into a toilet cubicle with me before school began on the first day of the summer term. 'Are you speaking to your dad yet?' she asked.

I sighed. The truth was, what had happened at Dad and Helena's engagement party probably hadn't *all* been his fault. But everything else that had happened up until then definitely was.

You'd think that after your dad decided that he was going to marry the most famous actress in the world, meaning that you suddenly have not only a future stepmum who has two Oscars sitting on her drinks cabinet but also a future stepsister who happens to be Britain's most well-known It Girl, your life would get a bit better.

But noooooo. Since Dad's sudden revelation last term I have:

1. Become the enemy of the most popular students in my year.

2. Accidentally tried to steal the Queen Bee's boyfriend.

3. Accidentally set her best friend on fire.

4. Been left hanging upside down in a waterfall in

front of my entire year, my Wolverine vest on full display.

5. Unintentionally become an It Girl in the press and almost lost my two best friends, Jess and Danny, when I attempted to use this to become more popular.

6. Sung *Fame!* in front of my WHOLE school, out of tune and with no backing music.

7. Fallen backwards into a plant pot, the video of which has now gone viral.

So yeah, you could say that Dad's surprise, very public engagement hadn't really helped my personal and emotional growth as a teenager.

And yes, it was pretty annoying of him to choose to have the party in Helena's house rather than a super-cool exclusive club somewhere in London. I mean, come on, he's marrying the most famous actress in the world and where do they choose to have their engagement party? At her home.

If you ask me, it's disappointing.

But still. I guess it wasn't not *technically* his fault that I fell into the plant pot. I don't even blame Helena for having Dracaena Lisa plants in her house. Some people might think them an unnecessary decoration for a hallway. And yes, some people might perhaps have thought to move them away from a space that guests might be gathering in.

But I have decided to overlook this lack of judgement. For my humiliation there really is only one person to blame: the person who invented sausage rolls.

I told Jess this.

'You're blaming sausage rolls?'

'No. Just the person who invented them,' I stated. 'I tried looking it up online. There's no one listed specifically, but I bet it was someone who owned a cat.'

Jess, for some reason, looked confused. 'What do cats have to do with anything? And why are we talking about sausage rolls?'

'Because,' I explained to her wearily, 'that's the whole reason we're in this mess in the first place!'

At the party, I had been happily listening to Marianne Montaine, my It Girl soon-to-be stepsister, wax lyrical about her hugely famous rock star boyfriend Tom Kyzer. But Dad forced me to come with him so he could introduce me to some of his old-person author friends. They weren't talking about interesting things like rock stars, either, just history and politics, which no one cares about really.

Luckily I spotted a waiter milling around with a platter of sausage rolls and an escape plan formed in my mind.

'Sorry,' I excused myself to no one in particular. 'I'm going to go get a sausage roll.'

The waiter had sped back towards the kitchen, though, so I followed him. But as I looked back over my shoulder to see if anyone was watching, he came back out with another big tray of sausage rolls. I swerved to avoid him, he yelped, I got scared by the yelp, lost my balance and fell back into the plant pot.

Jess blinked at me. 'And now you have a thing against sausage rolls?'

'The *inventor* of sausage rolls. The sausage rolls themselves were not at fault.'

'Well, it's a great story that makes no sense,' Jess nodded. 'Now can we get out of this cubicle? There really is not enough space in here for both of us.'

'But there are *people* out there.'

'Yeah, and I'm sure they're all desperate to hear the sausage-roll-plant-pot story.'

'Jess, be serious. It's all over the Internet. Everyone will be laughing at me. Again.'

'I'm sure they won't laugh. And if they do I'll tell them off.'

'Promise?'

'Yes.'

'OK, then,' I gave in. Jess opened the cubicle door and squeezed herself behind it while I shuffled nervously out towards the sink and checked the coast was clear. She followed me.

'Much better,' she sighed, putting her bag down again so she could run her fingers through her hair in front of the mirror. 'Now, what was I saying?'

As she spoke the door swung open and two girls from a couple of years below us came in chatting excitedly. They stopped as they saw us and then one of them hurriedly reached into her backpack, pulling out a notepad. 'Hi Anna,' she squeaked, coming nearer. 'Can you sign this for me?'

Jess smiled at me encouragingly. This girl couldn't be one of the four million people who had seen the plant-pot video.

'Of course,' I said in my most sophisticated voice, taking the pink sparkly pen that she offered and doing a swirly *AH* on the page.

'Thanks!' she giggled. 'You getting stuck in the plant pot was really funny.'

I shot a look at Jess. I was very much ready for this girl to get told off.

'It was *hilarious*, wasn't it?' Jess squealed – then she saw my face and stopped abruptly. 'But, er, not that funny.'

I pursed my lips and then, head held high, swept past the two girls out of the bathroom. As the door swung back I heard the first girl say, 'I'm putting this on eBay.'

'OK, so that wasn't the best telling-off I've given,' Jess admitted as she walked beside me along the corridor, 'but from now on I will be seriously cross if anyone even dares mention plant pots.' She patiently waited while I fiddled around with the code on my locker.

'Hey, anyone got any spare plant pots?'

I didn't give Danny the satisfaction of turning round.

'No, Danny,' Jess said sternly. 'That's not OK.'

'Hey,' he responded defensively. 'You're the one who told me that you've sent the video to your relatives in Canada.'

I looked at Jess accusingly. She held up her hands. 'That has definitely not happened. I have definitely not sent it to my four relatives in Canada and also a random second cousin in New Zealand.'

'Cheer up,' Danny said happily, giving me a nudge. 'It'll blow over.'

'Can it blow over quickly?' I hissed, my eyes darting towards a group of students with their eyes glued to a phone. They burst into laughter and looked up at me.

'You have way more important things to care about,' Jess said, a smile slowly expanding across her face. 'Like your boyfriend.'

I blushed furiously. 'Connor is not my boyfriend.'

'Maybe not yet, but you're a great match,' Jess said matter-of-factly. 'You're both kind of weird.'

'Did you see him lots over the holidays?' Danny asked as Jess ruffled his blond curls. He swatted her off.

'A little,' I said quietly, looking round to make sure he wasn't there. I still didn't know how Connor, the super-gorgeous, comic-drawing, perfect-in-every-way boy who made my hands go clammy just by smiling, still seemed to like me despite all the ridiculous things I had done last term. Well, I *thought* he still liked me . . . 'We saw some films.'

'Aaaaand?' Jess asked.

'And what?'

She sighed. 'I've only been asking you this question all holidays and you've been avoiding it. Don't think I haven't noticed.'

'I don't know what you're talking about,' I said, turning back to focus on the contents of my locker in the hope that Jess wouldn't make fun of how red my cheeks were going.

'Did you . . . *kiss*?'

'Jess!' I exclaimed, hitting the back of my head on my locker door, which had started swinging closed behind me.

'Well, did you, you smooth operator?' Jess laughed,

pushing the locker door back open for me as I rubbed my head.

'It didn't come up.'

Danny raised his eyebrows. 'I'm surprised at that.'

'Why?'

'You obviously like each other.' He shrugged. 'Still, I suppose you can't rush these things.'

'OK, Dr Casanova,' Jess snorted. 'Since when do you know anything about these things?'

'Casanova was not a doctor.' Danny rolled his eyes. 'What I meant was that Connor and Anna are both quite shy. Or, well, I guess I mean that Anna is quite socially awkward.'

'I am *not* socially awkward,' I protested.

They both looked at me.

'Anyway,' Jess cried. 'Why didn't Connor just lunge at you?'

'JESS!' I yelped, desperate for her to keep her voice down.

Despite my annoyance at Jess's lack of subtlety, it was actually a question I had been asking myself too. Connor and I hadn't seen much of each other during the Easter holidays. I'd had a bunch of things going on, including all of the celebrity events I now had to attend with Helena and Marianne, and Connor had been going to art lessons and working on his cartoon strip, *The Amazing It Girl*.

But still. There had been enough opportunities for him to, you know. Lunge at me.

'It's none of your business.' I fumbled for my books and shoved them in my bag.

'Oh please, it's always our business. You've been thinking about it, I can tell,' Jess teased.

'I have not. Well, maybe a little. It's just . . . do you think that . . . ?'

'Ahem.' Sophie Parker, the Queen Bee of Woodfield, had marched over with her ever-present sidekick Josie Graham. By the scowl on Josie's face, she clearly still hadn't forgiven me for setting her hair on fire last term.

'Hello, Anna,' Sophie said, coolly.

'Hi, Sophie, how was your Easter?'

'Great. I spent most of it with Brendan.'

I flinched. Brendan was the most popular boy in our school. In an attempt to prove my popularity last term I had accidentally (and temporarily) stolen him off Sophie. It was all sort of behind us now, though. Sort of. 'That's nice.'

'It is,' Josie sneered, from behind Sophie. 'Because she's Brendan's girlfriend, duh. And it's nice . . . being Brendan's girlfriend.'

Danny snorted.

'Thank you, Josie,' Sophie hissed back at her. Josie looked embarrassed.

'Miss Duke wants to see you in her office, Anna,' Sophie told me, looking at her perfectly-manicured nails. 'Pretty impressive, getting called to the headmistress's office on the first day of term. Oh, and don't forget to check out the list of events for sports day. I've put it up on the main noticeboard.'

'Sophie was asked by the Sports department to put it up first thing this morning,' Josie added as smugly as if Sophie had been asked to appear on the front cover of *Vogue*.

'I take it you'll be putting yourself forward to be team captain of the Puffins this year, Jess?' Sophie raised an eyebrow. 'Of course, there'll be no competition for me – I'm going to be leading the Eagles.'

'Actually, no,' Jess answered calmly as I looked at them all in confusion. Puffins? Eagles? Had my school turned into a bird sanctuary over Easter? How had I missed this? 'I want to put all of my focus on my Art project and my photography this term. So you don't need to worry about me waving the winner's trophy in your face when the Puffins win. I'm sure our captain will do the honours on my behalf.'

'Oh per-lease!' Sophie cackled. 'The Puffins haven't

beaten the Eagles in years! Everyone knows you don't have a chance. Besides,' she looked me up and down, 'it's not like the Puffins have the . . . best team this year. Anna, I know you're a Puffin. Good luck,' she smirked. 'I don't think there are any plant-pot assault courses so you might not fail in *every* event.' She turned on her heel and strode back down the hallway, with Josie laughing loudly next to her.

I looked at Jess in confusion.

'Oh, don't worry, I'll fill you in about sports day later.'

'Er . . . and the stern plant-pot telling-off you promised?'

'Damn it!'

What's wrong with you?

Nothing's wrong with me. I'm concentrating, Jess.

No one concentrates this hard while Miss Brockley writes on the board in a language no one on the planet understands.

Yes they do. She's writing important words that we need to know for our end of term exams. And some people on the planet do understand French.

Some people like who?

Well, I'm going to take a long shot and say that French people probably understand French.

Can you please tell me what's wrong with

you, so that we can hurry up and get to the bit where I tell you you're ridiculous and then you realise that it's actually fine? Are you worried about sports day? I told you I'd explain the whole Puffin thing to you. You don't need to worry, the school's just split into two teams.

Sounds weird to me — but no, I'm not worrying about sports day quite yet, although no doubt the fear will begin to loom soon.

Did Miss Duke say something weird? Was it something to do with the way you walk?

No, it wasn't a big deal, she just wanted to . . . Wait. What? What's wrong with my walk?

Nothing.

Jess! What is wrong with my walk?

Seriously, nothing. Stop passing notes. I'm concentrating.

Now I really am panicking. Why would you ask me if the headmistress wanted to see me about my walk?!

Geez, you're such a drama queen. You just walk a bit funny, that's all. Kind of . . . slumpy. I just wondered if she thought you had a problem or something that needed looking at. You know, in a caring way. Now tell me what's bothering you. You have a funny look on your face. Is it Connor?

Forget what I'm thinking about Connor, now all I can think about is my 'slumpy walk'.

Aha! So you were thinking about Connor! Spill.

It's nothing. I saw him this morning.

When?! What did he say???

When I came out of Miss Duke's office. I walked straight into them.

Them? Who is THEM?

I mean him. Him. I think Miss Brockley is looking this way. Wait, no, she's looking past me. Hah, she definitely is. I'm so stealthy at this. She's none the wiser. What a dodo. Anyway—

'What do you mean, you have detention?'

Why does Dad always have to make tiny things into such big deals? For example, that time when we went on holiday to the middle of nowhere in Ireland and as a joke I hid the hire car keys in a bush to make him panic. I couldn't have predicted that I wouldn't be able to remember which one I had hidden them in. I didn't stop hearing about that for days.

And now here he was all angry at me because I'd had the courtesy to ring him to tell him I'd be late home for supper.

'I got caught passing notes with Jess in French.'

'And they gave you detention? That seems pretty extreme,' Dad huffed. 'Let me come in and have a word with them.'

'In the note I called Miss Brockley a dodo for not realising I was passing notes.'

There was silence on the other end of the phone,

and then a long-drawn-out sigh.

'Fine. Come home straight afterwards, we have people round this evening.'

'Who do we have coming round? Actually, never mind,' I said hurriedly as Jess mouthed '*lunch*' at me. 'Got to go, Dad, see you at home.'

'Bye, Anna,' he said grumpily. 'Try not to insult too many teachers this afternoon.'

I rolled my eyes, said goodbye and then hung up before heading to the dining room.

'Why are you two always late?' Danny grumbled, coming up behind us.

'Duh, she's an It Girl,' Jess grinned. 'It's fashionable to be late. Anyway, Anna had to make a call.'

'Don't look too impressed,' I said as Danny raised his eyebrows at me. 'It was my dad.'

But as I sat down with my tray next to Danny I suddenly realised the whole room was staring at me and a spatter of giggles was coming from Sophie's table.

'What?' Jess asked them, hands on hips. 'Haven't any of you seen a celebrity before? Play it cool, guys.'

There was an uncomfortable pause, and then everyone started talking again. I smiled gratefully at Jess. 'Thanks.'

'Whatever,' she said, picking the mushrooms off her chicken. 'They were probably just staring because of your walk. Nothing to do with any plant pots.'

'Danny,' I said, 'do you think I walk funny?'

He shrugged. 'Maybe a little. Not really. I'm not sure I've noticed.'

'How *would* you describe Anna's walk?' Jess asked, picking up her glass of water. 'If you had to use a word to describe her walk, what would it be?'

'I don't know.' Danny looked thoughtful. 'Slumpy?'

'For goodness' sake!' I said as Jess raised her eyebrows victoriously at me. 'That's not even a thing!'

'It *is* a thing. You have a slumpy walk,' she said, with a smug I-told-you-so smile. 'Will you tell me about seeing Connor this morning?'

'Jess!' I glanced around me nervously. 'Stop talking about him so loudly.'

'He's not in here, I already checked.'

I craned my head to look carefully around the dining room. 'You're right. I wonder where he is.'

'You should know that,' Jess teased. 'He's your *boyfriend.*'

'How has your morning been, Danny?' I asked, attempting to change the conversation.

'Oh you know, the usual, teachers trying to frighten us with exam talk,' he sighed. 'I watched such a good nature programme last night though. Did you know that a scorpion will attract a mate by taking her pincers in his and then commencing a dance of courtship?'

'Well,' Jess looked bemused, 'that's interesting, Danny. Has Connor done that to you yet, Anna?'

'Done what?' I played with my food.

'Taken your pincers in his before commencing a dance of courtship.'

'We did dance together at the Beatus dance last term,' I shrugged.

'Yeah, but all of us were dancing together then,' Jess pointed out. 'And he was doing a meerkat impression. I'm not sure that counts as a dance of courtship. We'll have to consult Marianne. But tell us what happened with Connor this morning. You had such a weird face on in French class.'

'Nothing, really. We just talked.'

'No passionate kissing, then?'

'No, Jess! Outside Miss Duke's office is hardly a romantic setting,' I hissed. 'Stop talking about . . . *kissing* so loud! Imagine if someone heard you!'

Jess rolled her eyes but went quiet and Danny began to talk about scorpions again.

I was being honest: Connor and I *had* talked. But what I wasn't telling Jess was that it hadn't just been the two of us . . .

I was only in the headmistress's office for about thirty seconds. She'd wanted to check whether if I was OK after the whole me-stuck-in-a-plant-pot-being-an-Internet-sensation thing.

'You know . . .' Miss Duke began, no doubt wondering how she could possibly comfort me, '. . . these things blow over.'

'The Internet doesn't help that.'

'In this day and age I'm afraid that fame is a very difficult game.' She sat back in her chair thoughtfully, like a wise owl. Now that I think about it, her bright, round eyes and pointy features do kind of remind me of an owl.

'I'm not even sure *why* I'm famous. I haven't done anything except fall into a plant pot!' I shook my head. 'Seems unfair, really.'

'Well, if you feel like everything is getting too much for you,' Miss Duke looked at me kindly, 'my door is always open.'

I smiled at her and was getting up to leave, but she carried on.

'Except for Friday lunchtimes, when Mrs Ginnwell and I play Cluedo. I'm afraid my door is firmly closed then. I need all the concentration I can get.'

I almost laughed, but then I noticed her deadpan expression, so I just nodded and hurried out of the office.

That's when I saw Connor down the corridor. He was talking animatedly with a girl from our year, Stephanie. I didn't know her very well, and I definitely hadn't been aware that Connor knew her that well either, but clearly he did. She was laughing out loud and tossing her very shiny hair around glamorously. Why hadn't Connor ever mentioned being friends with her before?

Flustered, I turned round to walk the other way. But then Connor called out, 'Spidey!'

'Er, hi,' I said, turning around. I could feel myself blushing all the way down to my toes. Connor had called me 'Spidey' ever since last term, when he had discovered in detention that I shared his love of superheroes and all things comic book. I was usually teased for my Marvel comic-book obsession – especially by Jess, who continued to call it my 'weird, geeky Marvin habit', despite me correcting her a hundred billion times – but Connor didn't tease me one bit. He had even created a comic strip, called *The Amazing It Girl*, that was inspired by me. It was the nicest thing anyone had ever done for me.

'You're looking very furtive,' he grinned as he strolled up to me. 'Where have you been?'

'Miss Duke's office.'

'We haven't even got to the first lesson of term yet.' He

folded his arms and smiled cheekily. 'That's impressive, even for you, Anna.'

'She just wanted to, um . . . she wanted to check that I was OK. After the . . . plant pot incident.'

'Ah yes,' Connor nodded slowly, a look on his face that I couldn't quite work out.

Just then Stephanie and her impossibly shiny hair joined us. I saw that she had a cool, super short block fringe – I'd always wanted one and had considered cutting my long shaggy fringe shorter, but I knew I couldn't pull it off. Once I'd combed my hair forwards to see if it would give me a geek chic celebrity look. Dad walked in as I was doing it and asked, 'are you acting out *War Horse* again?'

I decided the look wasn't for me.

'Hi, Anna, did you have a nice holiday?' Stephanie asked.

'Um, yes, thank you. Not much happened,' I lied, hoping that she was the only person in the world who hadn't seen the plant pot video.

'I felt like I was working the whole time,' Stephanie said, rolling her eyes. 'So much revision!'

'Yeah, it wasn't fun,' Connor agreed. 'But there were some highlights.'

I felt a flutter in my tummy. Was he talking about hanging out with me? He must be! He had just been doing revision or Art class otherwise. Oh my goodness, Connor had referred to me as a HIGHLIGHT. I couldn't wait to tell Marianne and Jess!

'Well, you might call them highlights. But they were quite stressful as well!' Stephanie nudged Connor's arm.

Well, that was a little uncalled for, I thought. Hanging out with me hadn't been stressful! OK, fine, there had been *moments* of stress, like the time I got chased by a goose. But that only happened once and I was sure that Connor had just found it funny, not stressful.

'We learnt a lot,' Connor argued.

Very true. Next time, I was just going to surrender the bread to the goose.

'Maybe, but I still think I enjoyed the milkshake bar more.'

Wait. There definitely hadn't been a milkshake bar involved. What were they talking about?

'Milkshake bar?' I asked, as casually as possible.

'Sorry, Anna, I should have explained,' said Connor, turning to me. 'Stephanie was in those Art classes I went to, and after class a couple of times we went to this amazing milkshake bar. It does every flavour in the world.'

'You should come next time we go, Anna! Connor told me that you have a bit of a sweet tooth. They do Nutella flavour, and I know it's your favourite.' Stephanie smiled, hitching up all the books she was holding.

He'd told *her* about my Nutella love? I tried not to feel jealous of this girl who not only had very nice hair but was apparently artistic too, and who had spent her Easter holidays with Connor at a milkshake bar.

'I had a Nutella milkshake once in your honour,' Connor informed me proudly. 'It was pretty good.'

The bell rang, echoing down the near-empty corridor.

'Right, better get to class.' Connor hitched his bag on to his shoulder. 'Anyone walking this way?'

'I am,' Stephanie smiled.

Of course she was.

'I'm going the other way,' I said, in my most cheerful-not-minding voice.

'See you later, Spidey.' Connor smiled at me. 'I'll come find you.'

I nodded and walked away, glancing back to see Stephanie launching into what was probably another hilarious, sophisticated Art story that didn't involve anyone being chased by a vicious goose. But just as my heart was sinking, Connor looked back over his shoulder, catching my eye and smiling slowly, and the butterflies in my stomach went sugar-high crazy.

Jess can be very secretive.

While we were in detention that afternoon I could see that she was working on something, but annoyingly she wasn't sitting near enough for me to slip her a note as easily as we do in French. Mr Kenton had made us sit a couple of desks apart so we didn't distract each other.

Like that could stop me.

I screwed up a piece of paper tightly and tossed it towards her desk. I missed. Jess didn't look up.

'Psst!'

She still didn't look up. I saw how it was. Well, if it was OK for her to distract me and get us detention in the first place . . .

'PSST!'

Mr Kenton looked up, and I smiled innocently at him until he slowly looked back down at his book.

More inventive measures were clearly called for. I folded a paper airplane, wrote *pay attention!!!* on one of its wings and skilfully (I thought) hurled it into the air in Jess's direction.

It went straight up and then just plopped back down pathetically on to the ground by my feet.

I'm almost FIFTEEN and I can't even make paper airplanes.

In desperation, I threw a rubber at her head.

'What the . . . ?'

'Jess!' I whispered enthusiastically. 'It's me!'

'No kidding.' She rubbed the side of her head and gestured irritably around at the empty room. Somehow even Connor, who had been in detention all of last term for drawing comics and not concentrating, had escaped detention today.

'Are you practising French vocab?' I asked in a low voice, glancing warily at Mr Kenton.

'No.'

'Science?'

'No.'

'Is it English? Are you going over some notes for the exam?'

She shook her head. 'It's my Art project.'

'Geez!' I exclaimed, a little louder than I meant to. 'What is so good about Art?! I hear nothing else these days except for art, art, art!'

Mr Kenton looked up again and cleared his throat as

Jess looked bewildered. 'Miss Huntley, might I suggest you use this hour to actually do some work? I know that it's far more tempting to throw rubbers at the heads of your peers and rant about creative subjects, but this is detention. I can't bend *all* of the rules. I'm sure you have some homework to be getting on with?'

I nodded, flicking through some pages of notes and feigning interest in them until he went back to his book. Then I quietly tore out a piece of paper from my Chemistry book.

TOP SECRET

Jess, do you think Connor hasn't kissed me because I can't draw? WRITE BACK ASAP.

This time I got lucky. The scrunched-up ball landed on top of Jess's pencil case. She rolled her eyes at me. 'Read it!' I mouthed, glancing warily at Mr Kenton. Luckily, he was now engrossed in his novel.

I watched Jess as she opened it up, sighed and then wrote what I hoped was a sensitive and intuitive answer to my love-life woes. The paper whipped past my nose and skitted across the desk on my right. I reached over and eagerly opened it.

You're a loser.

When detention finally came to an end, Mr Kenton said, 'You know, Anna, you shouldn't let that YouTube video get you down. If anything, it's a lovely insight into the life of celebrities! I'm rather inspired to get a set of palm trees to frame my own staircase now. They add a certain *je ne sais quoi.*'

'Not a bad idea, Mr Kenton,' Jess nodded. 'Anna, maybe you should get Helena to put the palm trees on eBay! I bet you'd make a fortune.'

'Excellent business thinking, Jessica,' Mr Kenton said. 'Gold star!'

'They're not palm trees,' I cried, 'they're Dracaena Lisa plants!' And I flung my bag over my shoulder and flounced out the door.

'Word of advice, It Girl,' Jess grinned as she caught up with me, 'next time you make a witty comeback, try not to sound like the biggest nerd in the world. You just managed to make Mr Kenton look cooler than you.'

Note to self: kill Danny.

As we made our way towards the school gate, I caught sight of something that made my heart race about ten times faster than normal. Connor was standing right by it, rooting through his bag.

Jess sighed and shook her head as she noticed him. 'Seriously? You guys kind of disgust me, you're so cute.'

'What?' I played innocent.

'You said he wasn't your boyfriend! He's totally waiting for you.'

'Keep your voice down, Jess!' I hissed. 'He's *not* my boyfriend. He hasn't said anything about it and nothing's, you know, happened. We haven't even really been on a date, unless you count the goose incident.'

'Just lean in and kiss him, it's no big deal,' Jess said a little too loudly for my liking as we crossed the yard towards Connor.

'It *is* a big deal when you've never kissed anyone before. Anyway, stop talking, he'll hear us.'

'Hey guys,' Connor smiled, looking up as we reached him. 'How are you, Jess? How did the photography internship at the magazine go?'

'It was great!' said Jess cheerfully. 'I'll have to show you some of the work I did sometime. I've got to rush off now. See you guys tomorrow!' She gave me the most unsubtle wink I have ever seen and jogged away, grinning.

I was left blushing at Connor. Then my phone

beeped. 'Sorry,' I mumbled and dug around in my bag. I pulled it out.

SMOOCH TIME. Jx

Connor watched me, bemused, as I threw the phone back as if I'd been bitten. Did she have to use capslock?!

'You OK there, Spidey?' he asked.

'Yeah, just . . . um . . . someone annoying messaging me,' I sighed. 'Fans, you know how it is.'

'Sure.'

'And, um, how come you're still here?' I asked as innocently as I could, hoping he might say something like, *I'm madly in love with you and I wanted to wait for you to tell you that. Will you be my girlfriend for ever more?*

He shrugged. 'I was in the Art studio with Stephanie after school, doing a bit of planning for my Art project this term. I left, but then I thought I must have left my phone there, so I came back for it. I've just found it, though,' he said happily, tapping his bag. 'In here all along. Hey, this was great timing, I forgot you had detention.'

Oh.

'I'll walk you back home if you'd like? It's kind of on the way to mine, after all, and it's a nice day.'

'I'd *love* . . . er . . . like, er . . . that would be cool.'

41

'Right.' He grinned and pulled a bag of Milk Bottles out of his bag. 'So, how was detention without me?'

Distracted by my favourite sweets, I was relieved to find I could speak like a Normal Person again. 'It was fine. Not as entertaining as when you're there, though.'

He raised his eyebrows. 'You and Jess didn't just chat the entire time?'

'She's working on her Art project. And, you know, I've got lots of stuff to do. We were both pretty focused.'

'Right,' he chuckled. 'All that stuff you have to do.'

'Hey! I'm very busy and important, I'll have you know.'

'Oh, yes,' he said, suddenly serious. 'I forgot that you were Britain's favourite It Girl.'

'*Second*-favourite. Marianne is firmly in the lead, especially now that she and Tom Kyzer are a proper thing.'

'Does it feel weird that you're about to be the stepsister of someone who's dating a rock star?' he asked, looking at me quizzically and pushing back his dark hair from his eyes.

He was so nice to look at.

'Anna?'

Oh my god. I'd been STARING at him.

'Oh. Haha. Yes, well,' I mumbled trying to remember the question. 'I've only met Tom properly once, and my dad was so embarrassing then that I'm pretty sure

Marianne will never bring him round again.'

'Did your dad really ask him if he wanted to do a duet?'

'A *guitar* duet,' I sighed, recalling the moment in agony. 'He actually said, "back in the day I could have been a rock star myself." I almost died.'

'Your dad's amazing,' Connor said, shaking his head.

'Not when there's a rock star in your house and he's rummaging around in the attic for his old guitar. Then Helena told Tom the story about the time Marianne was little and she lifted her dress up in front of Madonna to show off her Disney pants, and I laughed so hard that I spilt my lemonade all over Tom's shoes. To top it off, Dog nicked his wallet off the table and chewed his bank card.' I bit my lip. 'I don't think any of us will be seeing Tom Kyzer any time soon.'

Connor laughed. 'I missed chatting to you properly over the holidays, Spidey.'

He stopped and I tripped over my own feet before I realised that he'd stopped because we'd reached my front door. He'd MISSED ME.

'I'll see you at school tomorrow then?' he asked.

'Yeah. I'm glad I survived today,' I chuckled nervously. 'Plant pot incident and everything.'

'Don't worry about that,' said Connor. 'People will get distracted by something else soon. Plus, I think the plant pot video was an excellent publicity stunt.'

'Connor, it wasn't a . . . I mean, I didn't do it on . . .'

'Anna,' he interrupted, winking at me. 'It was *an excellent publicity stunt* . . . I think the whole thing is pretty genius of you. It was a brilliant way of cheering the nation, getting more followers on social media and guaranteeing more support for anything you do in the future. So if anyone else asks, I'll say that it was an excellent publicity stunt.'

'Ohhhh,' I said, catching on at last. 'Yes, well. Not everyone can be a PR genius, but I try.'

'You do. Hey, we should have filmed the goose chase too. Your audience would have doubled with that one. Maybe we could pay the goose another visit?'

'Never!'

He laughed. 'Well, I'd better get going.'

'Yeah,' I replied, leaning back against my front door with my key in my hand and shuffling my feet.

There was a moment's silence. We caught each other's eye and Connor took a small step towards me. Considering he hadn't been standing too far away in the first place, this meant that he was *really* close all of a sudden. Close enough for my face to grow really hot. Close enough for me to forget to breathe. He reached out and his hand brushed my face. I started closing my eyes. I could hardly believe that it was actually happening. I was about to have my FIRST. EVER. KISS. *This was it.*

Except that, suddenly, the door was no longer behind me. I stumbled and fell backwards, landing with a thump on my bum.

Five reasons why the whole world should get rid of doors:

1. They are kind of pointless. I mean, what do they really do? If you think about it, they have no real function.

2. They might keep things out, but isn't that negative? Doors contribute to negative thinking. And we have enough negative thinking in the world already without doors.

3. Fingers can get caught in them. Doors are a danger to mankind.

4. People walk into them the whole time. Not only are doors a danger to mankind, but clearly we have not developed enough intelligence to handle their complex and cruel nature.

5. People are very irresponsible with them. Like when they just swing one open without checking to see if someone is leaning on the other side of it about to have their FIRST KISS.

'Anna, are you OK?' Connor's face popped into view as he knelt over me. I blinked up at him.

'Is there any chance that you didn't see that happen?'

His face broke into a look of relief and he chuckled. 'I didn't see a thing, I swear.' He reached out for my hand and gently pulled me up into a sitting position.

'Anna,' said my dad's voice. 'What's going on? Oh, hello Connor.'

'Hi, Mr Huntley,' said Connor.

Oh, brilliant. My dad was getting in on the act.

'Why are you on the floor?' Dad asked. 'Were you trying to salsa again? I told you the last time, it's just not the dance step for you.'

There it was. Things could *always* get worse.

'No, Dad, I was not trying to salsa.' I clambered to my feet and peered into the hall. Standing behind my dad were several men and women, all dressed in expensive-looking black tailored trouser suits. The men had their hair slicked back, while the girls had their hair in high, ridiculously-neat ponytails and sported bright red lipstick.

'Who are these strange people?' I looked round at them all. 'Er, no offence. I meant strange as in new. Not strange as in . . . strange. I'm sure you're all lovely. Whoever you are. Hello.'

Next to me, Connor sniggered and I elbowed him in the ribs.

'This is the wedding team.' Dad didn't sound too happy about it. 'But what happened to you, Anna?'

'Nothing! I fell through the door. What's a *wedding team*?'

'Anna! There you are, darling!' Helena breezed into the hall from the sitting room, looking very smart in a black knee-length dress and peach blazer. 'I thought I heard a commotion.'

'She fell through the door,' Dad informed her as she pulled me into a hug.

'Nice to see you, Miss Montaine,' said Connor politely.

'Connor, I've told you, call me Helena,' Helena gushed, embracing him dramatically. 'How is your Art going? Anna says you're the most talented artist she's ever seen.'

WAY TO PLAY IT COOL, HELENA.

'Um, did she?' asked Connor, sounding uncomfortable. 'Well, I've been going to some Art classes, so I think I'm getting better. I could show you some stuff next time I come over?'

'That would be simply fantastic, I just love art,' Helena declared, so enthusiastically it sounded as though she thought Connor was the next Picasso.

'If you're OK, Anna, then I should probably head

off,' Connor said, now looking like a rabbit caught in the headlights. 'I'll see you tomorrow?'

I opened my mouth to speak, but before I could say anything there was a loud crash from the sitting room, a shrill scream and an explosion of panicked voices shouting.

'What the . . . ?'

Suddenly about fifteen owls came flying towards us down the hall, flapping wildly.

'SHUT THE DOOR,' yelped one of the wedding team, and another threw himself courageously at the front door, slamming it closed just in time. Connor and I ducked as the owls, shut off from their escape route, were forced into a mass U-turn back towards the sitting room.

Then the wedding team leapt into action. They rushed away and reappeared wearing long, brown-leather gloves. The owls, noticing them, calmed and flapped over to them obediently.

'Gosh, how interesting,' Dad said weakly, patting himself down as he got up from his crouching position by the telephone table.

'What on EARTH is going on?' I demanded, completely bewildered.

'It's an idea for the wedding,' Dad said in a very, *very* strained voice.

'Don't you think it's precious?' Helena cooed, patting her hair.

'No, I don't think it's precious. There are OWLS casually flying around my house! Where's Dog? That could have been carnage!'

'One of the wedding team took him for a walk,' Helena explained as she led us all into the sitting room.

'YOU WHAT?' Letting Dog be taken for a walk by a STRANGER? That was completely unacceptable. What if someone stole him? It would be understandable – Dog is one of the most beautiful and intelligent creatures on this earth, after all. Also, Dog always gets sulky with me when other people take him on walks. It makes him think that Dad and I are neglecting him. Once, when Helena took him for a stroll because I was staying the night at Jess's house and Dad was on a tight deadline, Dog punished me by sneaking into my room and eating chapters one to ten of *The Hobbit*.

Dad looked at me apologetically. 'We had to get him out of the house while the owls were here. Helena insisted on seeing the birds herself. I made sure the dog walker was very trustworthy – Fenella assured me that he was very good with dogs.'

'Who is Fenella? What is going on? Why owls? Why has my house turned into Hogwarts?'

'Um, Anna?' Connor spoke up, patting my arm lightly. 'I really am going to have to head home now. Nice to see you again, Mr Huntley, er, Helena.'

He waved goodbye awkwardly. As the door shut behind him, I slapped my palm on my forehead. 'Well, that was mortifying. Dad, what is going *on*?'

Dad gestured dejectedly towards the sitting room and I marched past him to see for myself. I was greeted with what looked like a scene out of those totally random arty films that Dad loves: several empty owl cages, the wedding team standing around the room holding owls and clipboards, what appeared to be an extremely disgruntled bird handler sitting on the windowsill with his head in his hands, and Helena in a frenzied conversation with a woman who looked like she had walked out of the *Vogue* head office. Marianne was slumped back on a sofa fanning herself with a newspaper.

'Anna, come and meet Fenella,' Helena instructed jovially, leading the tall *Vogue* woman towards me. 'She's our wedding planner.'

'Yeah, hi.' I offered my hand, which Fenella took rather reluctantly. 'Why are there owls everywhere?'

'I thought we could have one carrying the ring. What do you think?' Helena clapped her hands excitedly.

'It's the stupidest idea of all time,' Marianne grumbled,

rubbing her forehead. 'Did you not just witness the chaos?'

'I told you not to let them all out at once,' the bird handler growled.

'What's the point in having birds if they can't fly about? I didn't realise they would go mental.' Marianne rolled her eyes. 'Anna, did you see them flying about everywhere? We can't have them at the wedding, they're completely wild.'

'Yeah, I did happen to notice them when they flew at CONNOR'S HEAD.' I sat down in a strop, pausing to accept the sparkling water that one of the wedding team offered me.

'Connor was here?' Marianne perked up at that.

'Connor is Anna's beau,' Helena explained to Fenella, who looked like she didn't care in the least.

'He is not my "beau"!' I groaned.

'I've told you this so many times, Mum. Stop using the word "beau",' Marianne instructed. 'You sound weird.'

'I am not weird!' Helena protested. An owl behind her made a loud hooting noise, prompting all the other owls to start hooting too. She glanced around. 'OK, fine, this is a slightly weird situation.'

'I think it is time we take our leave,' Fenella announced, and she clapped her hands three times.

The wedding team acted at once. They moved around the room at lighting speed, impressive considering their very tight black uniforms. They gathered together boxes of material and folders and rushed them outside to the line of black cars that I only noticed now were parked along our road.

'It looks like we're being investigated by the FBI,' Marianne observed as she pulled herself forwards to watch from the window. She was wearing a t-shirt with *I'm dating the band* on it.

'The FBI is American,' I corrected, spilling my sparkling water down my top and trying to act like nothing had happened.

'I'm glad that's over,' Dad said when the last owl had been carefully carried from the house and Dog had been returned, clearly very annoyed at not only missing out on whatever had left the strong bird-like scent in his house but also at being walked by a strange man. I knew it was Dad he was mad at – I saw him sniff agitatedly around before sitting his furry bottom down on Dad's reading glasses. Still, I ran upstairs when he wasn't looking and quickly moved all my books, just in case.

'No owls at the wedding,' Marianne stated firmly, looking at her mother.

'You're all very boring indeed,' Helena pouted.

Marianne ignored her. 'So, Anna, how was it with Connor?'

'What do you mean?'

'Oh come on,' Marianne grinned. 'Are you guys properly together at last, or are you still playing it cool?'

'I think her coolness factor went out the window when she fell through the door,' Dad observed.

I narrowed my eyes at him. 'Coming from the man who writes books about tanks and sings Disney songs in the shower?'

That shut him up.

'You fell through the door? Anna!' Marianne said, throwing up her arms and causing all of the bangles around her wrists to jangle loudly. 'Why do you keep falling over all the time? What's wrong with you?'

'Nothing! I was leaning against the stupid door and someone opened it for no reason.' I looked accusingly at Helena. 'Someone from the *wedding team*. What even is a wedding team?'

'They're putting the wedding together for us,' Helena explained, flicking through a bridal magazine. 'I make all the decisions, they do all the work.'

'*We* make all the decisions,' Dad corrected. Helena ignored him, engrossed by a feature on cake.

'Why were you leaning against the door?' Marianne

asked. 'Why weren't you just opening it?'

'Because . . . we were chatting.' I shrugged and kicked off my shoes. 'I'm going to go upstairs and change.'

'Oh my goodness,' Marianne gasped. 'Was he about to kiss you?'

'What? No!' I blushed furiously.

'He totally was! You've gone bright red!' She squealed. 'You *guys*!'

'No, he wasn't. We were *chatting*,' I explained to the room. 'There was no kissing, or attempted kissing.'

'I should hope not,' Dad went all huffily. 'You're only fourteen.'

'Oh Nick.' Marianne looked at him sympathetically. 'You're so naive.'

'Look, there was no kissing and there probably never will be,' I announced, standing up. 'Everyone at school has seen the plant pot video. Including Connor.'

'Connor doesn't care about plant pots,' Marianne said smugly. 'He's just *potty* about you.'

'Very nice, how long have you been waiting to say that?'

'Basically since the video went viral. But I needed the right moment. Don't worry about it, he'll kiss you soon enough.' Marianne winked.

'Not under my roof. And I think Anna's mother

would agree with me too,' Dad added.

Marianne snorted. I knew what she meant. My mum and dad had never actually been married, or even really together, and they were both very happy with this arrangement. Mum was what you might call a free spirit, and me kissing a boy was something I suspected she would have been delighted at, especially as she kept telling her friends that, unlike her, I was a 'late bloomer'. Mortifying. She and Helena were just as bad as each other when it came to the topic of my barely-existent love life.

'Everyone!' Helena suddenly exclaimed from where she was perched on the end of the sofa. She held up her magazine for us all to see. 'How do we all feel about exploding cakes?'

From: jess.delby@zingmail.co.uk
To: anna_huntley@zingmail.co.uk
Subject: YAWN

OK, where are you? It does NOT take this long to walk back to your house, even if you're distracted by . . . oh, I don't know . . . KISSING A BOY????

Come on. Spill. And make it snappy. Mum keeps yelling

at me because she can't find the power button on the TV controller.

J x

From: anna_huntley@zingmail.co.uk
To: jess.delby@zingmail.co.uk
Subject: Re: YAWN

There was no kissing. I fell through the front door.

Love, me xxx

From: jess.delby@zingmail.co.uk
To: anna_huntley@zingmail.co.uk
Subject: Wow

You fell through the front door. Seriously?

What is wrong with you?

J x

From: anna_huntley@zingmail.co.uk
To: jess.delby@zingmail.co.uk

Subject: Re: Wow

I've been asking myself that question a lot this evening.

Love, me xxx

It Girls or Twit Girls?

British socialites are overpaid and overrated. Tanya Briers on why It Girls are on their way out.

They are always on our front pages and our screens and they always pose one simple question: what exactly are they famous for? I am, of course, referring to 'It Girls', the 'lucky' few who find themselves in the limelight, engulfing our social media and news updates with their attention-seeking outings and ridiculous opinions without ever actually doing anything.

The likes of **Cecily Bright, Marianne Montaine** *and, newest to the game,* **Anna Huntley**, *make me weep for the state of our nation. What have they achieved to deserve such press coverage? Why should we read about them? These are not role models for the new generation. Do we want young girls to aspire to be someone like* **Miss Huntley** *(watch Anna Huntley's plant pot mishap by* **clicking here***), whose only claim to fame appears to be her father's impending marriage to Helena Montaine – and, oh yes, that plant pot incident.*

We need to rebel against this new era of celebrity. Let's revolt against the It Girl!

'Do you think they've all read it?' I asked nervously from the car on the way to school the next morning.

Marianne removed her sunglasses and peered over at everyone standing outside school, waiting for the bell to go. 'I don't know, Anna. Maybe? It got a lot of attention. Tanya Briers is a big name, and your video didn't help.'

'It's in the all time top ten most watched videos on YouTube now.'

Marianne nodded gravely. 'But you still have to go to school, kid.'

'They'll destroy me. Sophie is going to have a field day. She's probably set the article as the background on her phone already.'

'So? Who cares?'

'I care! You sound like Dad.'

'Anna.' Marianne swivelled in her car seat, angling herself towards me. 'I thought you were used to this kind of thing by now. It's just what happens when you're . . . you know . . .'

'An It Girl?' I sighed. 'She's right, you know.'

'Who's right?'

'Tanya.'

'What are you talking about?'

'What am I famous for, Marianne? Nothing! I'm not famous for anything!'

'You never set out to be famous, Anna! Everyone knows that it just happened to you. You can't believe a word Tanya says. You're a wonderful person and a great role model. It's important that you get that into your head before the press conference next week.'

'I don't see why I have to go to that,' I stropped. 'It's a book about Helena, it has nothing to do with me. She didn't even write it, it's just a stupid biography. She must have a million out there written about her.'

'We're going as a family,' Marianne said firmly. She slid her sunglasses back on. 'Because that's what we're about to be. It will be lots of fun. Now get out of the car, I've got to go to a photoshoot.'

I pursed my lips and then lifted myself out of the passenger seat.

'Anna, remember,' Marianne wound down the window. 'You're a great role model.'

'Marianne, just this morning I realised that over Easter I accidentally put Dog's shampoo in my shower and my shampoo in the dog cupboard. I've been using dog shampoo for three weeks.'

Marianne stared at me in amazement and then turned

the keys in the ignition. 'Yeah, OK, you're pretty tragic. Have fun at school!'

The first thing I knew I had to do was speak to Connor. Now that I had fallen into a plant pot, AND fallen through a door, AND been labelled a waste of space by the British press, I figured he might not be thinking that highly of me. So I needed to reassure him that, you know, I was a Normal Person – or at least fool him for a while.

I got safely into the school without anyone yelling anything mean and went to lean casually next to Connor's locker, like I just happened to be stopping there because I was tired.

Hovering, by the way, is easier said than done – especially when people keep opening the locker doors on which you are nonchalantly trying to lean. I had to keep shuffling about every time someone huffed about needing to get into one.

By the time Jess and Danny came past, I'd given up on all attempts to be casual. Instead I was stood bolt upright, wedged firmly between two open locker doors. Jess stopped in her tracks and raised her eyebrows. 'Anna. What are you doing?'

'What does it look like?'

'It looks like you're stuck.'

'Please. I am not stuck.'

The student to the left of me swung his locker door closed, yanking out some of my hairs that had been caught in the lock. I yelped.

'Seriously, what are you doing?' Danny asked.

'Hanging out,' I shrugged, rubbing my head where it was sore. 'Casually.'

'Wait.' Jess's eyes widened. 'Isn't this . . . Connor's locker?'

'Is it? Oh, yeah, maybe.'

Jess rolled her eyes. 'OK, you're hilarious. It's fine if you're waiting for him. You don't have to try and play it cool in front of us.'

'I'm not playing it cool,' I mumbled. 'I was just resting against this locker and waiting for you guys. You know, to go into assembly.'

'Oh, really?' The corners of Danny's lips twitched as he tried (not very hard) to suppress a smile. 'Lucky we spotted you, then.'

'Yes, it is lucky.' I picked up my bag. 'Shall we?'

'Are you OK, by the way?' Jess asked, her forehead furrowing. 'I read what Tanya Briers wrote about you.'

'You know that article is all a load of rubbish, right?' Danny added.

'Guys, I'm fine,' I lied. 'Honest.'

'If it means anything,' Jess hooked her arm through mine, 'I think you're exactly the kind of person that girls should be looking up to.'

'Me too,' Danny huffed. 'That Tanya woman is just trying to get noticed. It's all trash.'

'Well, Tanya Briers certainly achieved her aim. You can't miss her. Her opinion seems to be splashed about everywhere.'

'Personally, I think it's flattering that you're even mentioned. Right, Danny?' Jess pinched him.

'Oh, yeah, definitely. There are loads of It Girls out there who . . . uh . . . who weren't mentioned. Any publicity is good publicity.'

'Whatever, let's change the subject,' I said, gloomily. Not only was this conversation depressing, it was clear that Connor wasn't going to come to his locker before assembly.

'Good plan. So, who wants to bet that Sophie makes sure that she's centre of attention this term when she becomes a team captain for sports day?' Jess smirked. 'She makes me glad I'm not an Eagle, even if they do win every year.'

'Can someone please explain this bird thing? Puffins? Eagles? What are you talking about?' I asked as they both burst out laughing.

'Sorry, Anna,' Jess laughed as we walked into the assembly hall and sat down. I craned round to try and spot Connor, but he didn't seem to be here either. I tried to bury my disappointment and listen to what Jess was telling me. 'I've been meaning to explain it to you. For sports day the school is divided into the Eagles and the Puffins. The Eagles win every year and the Puffins, well, we always lose.'

'How do you get selected for a team?'

'It's random,' Danny took over, leaning round Jess to fill me in. 'But for some reason the Eagles seem to win each year. It's probably because you stay on the same team all the way through school.'

'The Sports department also chooses a captain for each team in the summer term,' Jess added. 'This time, it will be two people from our year. If someone really wants to do it they can nominate themselves, otherwise someone is picked randomly.' She eyed up Sophie who was chattering loudly to a group of girls in the front row. 'You can guess who'll be putting herself forward as captain of the Eagles. But I'm not being Puffin captain – the captains have to take part in at least four events, including the relay final, plus they have to be on hand for team morale.' She waved her hand. 'I really want to focus on my Art project this year. James Tyndale will probably go for it. He's sportier than me anyway.'

'James Tyndale is a Puffin?' I asked curiously, spotting James in the popular group as he joked around with Brendan Dakers, along the row from Sophie. 'Isn't he with Brendan and Sophie?'

Even though I had spent a lot of time with the popular group last term, when Brendan Dakers had thought that as a newly titled It Girl I should be hanging out with them, I had never actually really got to know James.

'Like I said, it's randomly selected, not based on who your friends are,' Danny reminded me.

'James would make a good captain,' Jess nodded.

'You're only saying that because you want to stare at him in his running shorts all day,' Danny teased.

'Yup!'

'Jess, do you fancy James Tyndale?!'

'Not in the slightest,' Jess declared. 'I couldn't properly fancy anyone who's part of that crowd. They think they're better than everyone else. But you can't deny that he is hot.'

'Hot?'

'Come on! He's not bad looking,' Jess said, and all three of us watched as James rolled his eyes at something Brendan was saying. 'Everyone gets distracted by Brendan's boy-band looks – as you know, Anna.'

'Oh, cheers.' I shifted uncomfortably at the memory of last term's disastrous crush on Brendan Dakers.

'Just joking,' she grinned. 'But look at James! That tall, broad frame, that manly jaw, those bright green eyes framed by heavy eyebrows.'

'Gross, you two. Can we stop leching on boys now? I'm still here, you know.' Danny looked slightly green.

'I'm glad we're all Puffins,' Jess said. 'Can you imagine being under the reign of Sophie? Bleugh.'

'Being bossed around by Sophie would probably make sports day even worse,' I admitted.

'I should have guessed you'd hate sports day,' Danny grinned. 'Come on, it's not that bad.'

It was time to put them straight.

Reasons why sports day should be optional:

1. It's a day of torture for anyone who is not sporty.

2. If you are not sporty, everyone witnesses how non-sporty you are – it is literally a day that puts your failure on show.

3. Then you come last . . .

4. . . . at everything.

5. Seriously, not one thing do you not come last at.

6. If school makes a day of sports compulsory then they should make a day of everything else compulsory too, so that sporty people know

how it feels to be publicly mocked.

7. Although I would also come last at drama or music too, so maybe that's not the best idea.

8. What is even the point of athletics? Why do we need to jump into a pit of sand? Or over a pole? And hurdles! Why is there so much running? WHERE ARE WE RUNNING TO?

'Wow,' Jess whispered. 'I don't think I've ever seen you so passionate about anything before.'

'Yeah, you have,' Danny said. 'Remember a couple of weeks ago when she couldn't open that packet of bacon-flavoured crisps and she threw them at the wall in a rage? She was pretty passionate then.'

Thank goodness Tanya Briers didn't interview any of my friends.

From: anna_huntley@zingmail.co.uk
To: marianne@montaines.co.uk
Subject: TOP SECRET

OK, so I need your advice. But DON'T TELL ANYONE.

So you know how . . . um . . . you know how I like Connor? In *that* way? (Do you know what I mean? Tell me if you need to explain this.)

I was thinking about it and I realised that there's no way he's going to want to date me now, with the whole plant pot thing and the article. He must be thinking, *why would I date someone who is bad at everything and famous for nothing?*

That's why I've hardly seen him since we got back to school, right? And he's not going to want to take me to a milkshake bar if he's thinking that.

So I tried to make a list of all the things I'm good at that make me dateable and this is what I've come up with so far:

Things that I am good at:

1.

As you can see, I haven't got very far, so I just wondered if you might want to contribute in any way.

Love, me xxx

PS You should know that I spent an hour working on the above list.

PPS You should also know that I am going to spend the rest of the evening crying in the shower.

From: marianne@montaines.co.uk
To: rebecca.blythe@bouncemail.co.uk; helena@
montaines.co.uk
Subject: FW: TOP SECRET

You two have to read this. This calls for emergency measures.

From: rebecca.blythe@bouncemail.co.uk
To: anna_huntley@zingmail.co.uk; marianne@montaines.co.uk; helena@montaines.co.uk
Subject: Re: TOP SECRET

Darling, there are hundreds of things you're good at! What about your duck impression? You know, when you do that cute little waddle? That should be number one on your list.

Really, I've never seen anyone impersonate a duck quite so well.

Mum xxx

From: helena@montaines.co.uk
To: anna_huntley@zingmail.co.uk; marianne@montaines.co.uk; rebecca.blythe@bouncemail.co.uk
Subject: Re: TOP SECRET

And you almost taught Dog to give a paw, didn't you? I know he didn't quite catch on but he was so nearly there with that one! Very impressive, I thought.

So there's another one, you're good at teaching dogs tricks!

Helena x

From: rebecca.blythe@bouncemail.co.uk
To: anna_huntley@zingmail.co.uk; marianne@
montaines.co.uk; helena@montaines.co.uk
Subject: Re: TOP SECRET

Very good point, Helena! Right, let's see, so now we
have . . .

Things Anna is good at:

1. Her simply uncanny duck impression

2. She can (almost) teach dogs tricks

What about sarcasm? She's very good at being sarcastic.
She gets that from her father.

Rebecca x

From: helena@montaines.co.uk

To: anna_huntley@zingmail.co.uk; marianne@
montaines.co.uk; rebecca.blythe@bouncemail.co.uk
Subject: Re: TOP SECRET

Do you know, I think Nick's got more sarcastic recently? He made a very rude comment about our wedding the other day. God forbid I should mention a tower of macarons.

Helena x

From: rebecca.blythe@bouncemail.co.uk
To: anna_huntley@zingmail.co.uk; marianne@
montaines.co.uk; helena@montaines.co.uk
Subject: Re: TOP SECRET

Well, in my personal opinion, Helena, no wedding is complete without a tower of macarons.

Shall we review the list?

Rebecca x

From: helena@montaines.co.uk
To: anna_huntley@zingmail.co.uk; marianne@
montaines.co.uk; rebecca.blythe@bouncemail.co.uk

Subject: Re: TOP SECRET

Yes, let's. You do the honours, Rebecca. With such a list shaping up, I would certainly get in line to date you, Anna, if I were a teenage hunk!

Helena x

From: rebecca.blythe@bouncemail.co.uk
To: anna_huntley@zingmail.co.uk; marianne@
montaines.co.uk; helena@montaines.co.uk
Subject: Re: TOP SECRET

Things Anna is good at

1. Her simply uncanny duck impression

2. She can (almost) teach dogs tricks

3. She is good at being sarcastic

There now, Anna! I'm sure you're feeling all better about everything. I'm glad we could help.

Lots of love,

Mum xxx

From: anna_huntley@zingmail.co.uk
To: marianne@montaines.co.uk
Subject: Re: TOP SECRET

I hate you.

From: marianne@montaines.co.uk
To: anna_huntley@zingmail.co.uk
Subject: Re: TOP SECRET

In my defence, I had genuinely forgotten how weird they
both were.

'I've got it!' Jess cried, pouncing on me as I walked across
the school yard that afternoon.

'Got what? Can you keep your voice down? I'm trying
not to attract too much attention these days.'

'Anna, you're getting fan mail from plant enthusiasts
in Peru,' Jess scoffed. 'I don't think you could stay under
the radar right now. Anyway, I've come up with a cunning
plan.'

'Is it moving to Antarctica?' I asked, wearily climbing

the school steps as she bounded alongside me.

'No, it's way better. You should invite Connor to the press conference! You know, that one for the book about Helena!'

'Are you mad? Jess, how many pop tarts have you eaten this morning?'

'It's completely genius,' Jess told me, in a slightly more hushed tone as we entered the confines of the main school building. 'You take him to the press conference, you get photographed together, you look beautiful and sophisticated and then . . . BAM!'

I yelped as she thrust herself forwards, bringing me to a sudden stop.

'Smooch-town.'

'*Smooch-town*?'

'Yes, Anna,' she nodded, allowing me to begin walking again. 'Smooch-town.'

'You think that if I invite Connor to a press conference with my whole family, he'll think it's the perfect time to kiss me?' I sighed. 'Jess, you're deluded.'

'Like I say, you'll look super sophisticated that evening. That'll give you a confidence boost.'

'Jess, I hate to break it to you, but I –'

Then we reached my locker door and I was stunned into silence. Stuck up on it was the article by Tanya Briers, with certain parts highlighted and starred. At the bottom of it someone had written in black marker pen: 'LOSER!'

Jess took a deep breath and yanked it off my locker, scrunching it up and lobbing it at the bin. 'Morons,' she muttered. 'Looks like the work of the Queen Bee's minions.'

'You don't *know* that, and it doesn't matter anyway. Tanya *is* right. I'm useless at everything except making a fool of myself. The best talent that my mum could list was a duck impression.'

'You have a duck impression?'

'It really is excellent, I can't lie.'

'Look, Anna, you're forgetting the big picture here because of one stupid article. Invite Connor to the press conference, have your first kiss and after that you won't care whether you're good at things or not.' Jess sighed. 'Anna, you have to stop cowering. You've got to seize the moment!'

'I guess I could . . . see if he wanted to come.'

'That's my girl!' Jess punched my shoulder playfully. 'Ask him after school. He's in the Art department at the moment.'

'What's he doing there?'

'His art project. He's working on it with Stephanie.'

'Him and Stephanie? Together? Really?'

'Yeah,' Jess shrugged. 'She's pretty amazing at art. Have you seen her stuff?'

I shook my head. And despite the fact she didn't stop for breath as we headed towards our first lesson of the day, I didn't hear a word Jess said after that.

I knew now that Jess was right. I really would have to seize the moment with Connor . . . before someone else did.

He said yes. Granted, he sounded a little quiet on the phone, but I was so nervous that every second where I wasn't speaking (and there weren't many) seemed like a lifetime. Maybe I'd just imagined it.

Still, I was so excited when I got off the phone that I went straight into a victory dance with Dog. I hadn't been rejected! He'd rather spend an evening with me than have another arty milkshake bonanza with Stephanie and her block fringe.

Dog was thrilled by the spontaneous dance-off, especially when Michael Jackson started blasting out of the radio. Dog loves him. In fact, he got so overexcited midway through 'Black or White' that he left me doing the Worm and zoomed off to the kitchen. He returned with the blender and, when I tried to take it off him, went on a wild and triumphant victory lap round the house, crashing into the drinks cabinet as he did so.

But as Dog continued his blender adventure, Dad in hot pursuit and bellowing at the top of his lungs, the reality of my press conference date with Connor began to dawn on me. My emotional journey went as follows:

1. Smug. Connor wanted to hang out with me rather than Stephanie!

2. Slightly worried. I would be spending an entire evening with him.

3. Quite nervous. Potentially I might end up kissing him.

4. Totally freaked out. The whole situation was ridiculous!

5. Completely terrified. There was no way I was going to be able to go.

'Of *course* you have to go,' Jess chuckled on the afternoon of the conference, fiddling with a setting on her camera. She had come over to help me prepare. 'Helena would be so upset if you weren't there.'

'And so would I!' said Marianne, looking horrified.

'But –'

'No buts, Anna, you're coming. Now, try this one on. Connor won't be able to resist smooching you once he sees you in this!' Marianne shoved a dress in my face while Jess took a picture.

'Hey! You didn't ask me to smile or anything,' I protested as Jess twisted the lens and took another.

'And will you both stop saying "smooching"!'

Jess and Marianne grinned at each other.

'How's the photography coming on?' Marianne asked Jess as she picked her way through the line of heels that her stylist, Cat, had brought over for me. Of course, Marianne had picked out her own outfit weeks ago.

'Great, thanks,' Jess smiled, taking some snaps of my room, which currently looked like a magazine's discarded fashion cupboard. There were clothes and shoes everywhere. 'I'm actually doing a photography project for my Art exam.'

'That's cool, what on?' Marianne zipped me in and stood back to look at me. 'No. Take it off. You look like the Cookie Monster. OK, try these jeans with this top.'

'I'm not sure yet,' Jess answered with a grin. I could tell she was enjoying being around to witness Marianne boss me about. 'I did have an idea, but actually I think I might change it. A wave of inspiration hit me the other day.'

'Ah, well, go with your gut,' Marianne advised. 'Good Lord no, Anna, take those off. You look like David Bowie.' I burst out laughing and heard the familiar click of Jess's camera.

I've never really been a fan of the paparazzi. All those flashbulbs go off in my face and blind me, so I end up walking in circles for about five minutes afterwards with blotches across my vision. But when we arrived at the press conference, for the first time ever, I didn't want the photographers to stop.

That's because as we pulled up outside the hotel where the event was being held and I got out of the car, the paparazzi surged forward and security stepped in, holding them back as they pushed against the rope. Instinctively, Connor took my hand.

HE TOOK MY HAND.

I think I actually stopped breathing.

I gripped it tightly, concentrating my hardest on not having sweaty palms as we were led towards the door. Having photographers stand in my way has never really been my thing, but with Connor holding my hand as though it was the most natural thing to do, I was thrilled.

Once we were out of the chaos and safely into the grand entrance hall, the quiet was almost deafening in comparison. I smiled nervously at him. He wasn't letting go of my hand.

'Whoa,' he breathed. 'Is it always like that?'

'Not really. You usually have a lot more space on the red carpet.' I crinkled my nose. 'Wow, never thought I'd be saying sentences like that one.'

'Yeah, must still be a bit strange.' He looked quite

serious suddenly, and held my hand even tighter. 'Spidey, you know, before all of *this* happened,' he waved round at the glamorous hall, a huge poster of Helena's book on a gilt frame outside the room we were about to go into. 'I –'

Just then a lady in a black pencil skirt suit bustled over to take our coats and ushered us through the door, into a room buzzing with the sound of almost a hundred people chatting loudly and clinking glasses. Everyone was mingling around the rows of chairs that had been set out for when the questions began. Nobody paid much attention to Connor and me as we came in, but when Helena swanned through the doorway behind us there were gasps of admiration and a spatter of applause. She went straight up to the first group of people to greet them with air kisses.

Connor looked at me and gestured to a quiet corner of the room, away from Helena's admirers. There was a red-velvet chaise longue thing there, just like the ones you see in old Hollywood movies.

Connor sat down next to me. 'Wow, it's non-stop.'

I nodded. 'It always is, these days!'

He looked at me, his head tilted thoughtfully. 'So I read that article about It Girls . . . it made me so angry.'

'Thanks,' I said happily, my heart swelling. Was this what he was going to say before, in the hallway? I could feel myself blush. He sounded so protective.

'Yeah, really angry,' he said, pushing his hair back away from his face. 'Who cares that you're not famous for *something*? You didn't ask for that article to be written about you!'

Wait, what?

Oh, no. Connor had just admitted that he thought I wasn't good at anything! I didn't want him to like me *in spite* of the fact that I was a talentless loser. I wanted him to really *believe* that I wasn't!

Would I really have to pull out the duck impression just to prove that I could do SOMETHING?

But before I could ask, I was pounced on by a very beautiful but clearly flustered PR girl. 'So this is where you've been hiding!' she cried, pushing her glasses up her pretty nose. 'Come on, you need to be at the table with Helena and your family. Come with me!'

I turned and looked apologetically at Connor, who shook his head with a smile to show it was OK. 'Quick, quick, you can come back to that gorgeous boy later,' she chastised me, rushing me to the front of the room. By the time I had sat down next to Marianne, with Helena and my dad on her other side, I couldn't even see Connor in the crowd any more, just eager journalists leaning forward and bright lights shining in our direction. He'd probably gone off to find more interesting people to talk to. You know, people with actual talents.

'Let's start with you, Fran,' Helena's publicist announced, smiling at a journalist in the front row. The questions began firing and I zoned out. Despite being right in the middle of it, I actually missed most of the press conference – and this is why:

1. None of the questions were directed at me.

2. I got distracted by the fact that Connor knew I wasn't good at anything. He was definitely going to be more interested in someone like Stephanie who actually had at least one talent – a real talent, not just a duck impression.

3. I got distracted by a guy who had a hat with a weird swirly pattern on it.

4. I got distracted by a bug landing in my glass of water.

5. I got distracted by knocking over my glass of water when I tried to get the bug out.

6. I got distracted by the person who came to hand me a napkin to mop up the water I'd spilt.

7. I got distracted by the stern look my father shot at me down the table because I was distracting everyone.

8. I got distracted by the fact that the bug was

STILL flying about in my face.

But then one question got my full attention.

It was asked by a middle-aged man near the back, who stood up when he was chosen. 'I have a question for Marianne and Anna,' he boomed, scratching his bristly beard. 'What do you both think about Tanya Briers' recent article about the pointlessness of It Girls? Do you have any comments on the fact that people think that you're bad role models for young women?'

'They have no comment on that,' Helena's publicist barked, glancing around to select the next question. But the man didn't give up that easily.

'You two don't have anything to say about the fact that you've been publicly labelled as a waste of space?'

'She didn't use those words, I believe,' Marianne snapped. The journalist smiled – she had taken the bait.

'She certainly implied as much. What do you have to say to your critics, especially Tanya Briers? Marianne, you have been accused of being famous for nothing other than partying and spending money. Do you have anything to say about that?'

'Marianne doesn't do nothing,' I piped up, furious with him. Who was this guy? I hated his horrible beard. 'She works very hard.'

'Really? Doing what?'

'Aside from raising awareness about good causes, she has plenty of personal projects going on.' Marianne squeezed my hand gratefully under the table and I saw Helena place a hand on her heart, looking extremely proud. Dad looked wary.

'OK,' the journalist said, scribbling something on his notepad. I picked up my glass of water, congratulating myself for handling him so well and sticking up for Marianne. 'And what about you, Anna?'

I paused, the glass halfway to my mouth. The room was deadly silent. 'Excuse me?' I squeaked.

'What are you famous for? Why should you be a role model to the young girls of this country?'

I glanced up at the sea of faces and spotted Connor for the first time. He was sitting at the back, watching me intently, his forehead furrowed. His earlier words swirled round my head: *who cares if you're not famous for something? You're not famous for something, you're not famous for something, you're not famous for something, you're not famous for something . . .*

'I . . . um . . .'

'Only questions about the book, please!' The publicist attempted to restore order, but the journalist pushed on. Now he had everyone's attention. They all wanted to hear what he was going to say next.

'Why should girls look up to you? What is it that you inspire?'

'Well, I guess that I –' I mumbled.

'You have no right –' Marianne began angrily.

'Your dad is getting married to an actress,' he snorted. 'But one could argue, much like Tanya Briers has done, that technically *you* haven't done anything noteworthy in your entire life. Right?'

I closed my mouth. There was nothing I could think of to say.

'Enough questions!' Helena's publicist looked flustered and turned to whisper hurriedly at some of her colleagues standing near her. They nodded. 'That brings us to the end of the Q&A. Helena, if you would like to give us your closing statement?'

I was in such a daze that I didn't hear a word of it. When she finished, there was a polite round of applause, and then the room became filled with conversation. I knew that social media would already be buzzing with the It Girl fame debate.

The rest of the evening was a blur. I barely got to say goodbye to Connor, and my heart sank. Dad had thought it best to head home as soon as possible, leaving Helena's publicity team to arrange a separate car for him. I tried to apologise as I was bustled away but I'm not sure he even heard me.

When we got into our car, there was an uncomfortable silence.

'I think the book will sell well,' Dad said to Helena at last, sounding strained.

'Yes,' she answered automatically, but she was looking at me in concern.

'Anna, are you OK?' Marianne asked, taking my hand and squeezing it. I nodded.

'I hope that journalist is crossed off the list from now on. How dare he speak like that to a fourteen-year-old?' Dad growled, clenching his fist.

'Ignore him,' Helena instructed. 'Just ignore him.'

'But,' I said softly, 'he's right. Just like Tanya Briers is right. What am I famous for?'

They all looked at each other. I knew we were all thinking the same thing, though no one was brave enough to say it: *nothing*. I was famous for nothing.

'You're joking, right?' asked Marianne. She looked at me, trying to get me to agree. I didn't say anything. We were standing in a stable yard on the afternoon of the day after the awful press conference, looking at Helena's latest wedding idea – horses. Apparently, as well as the owls and the exploding cakes, Marianne and I were going to arrive at the church on horseback.

'You don't like them?' Helena asked, looking hurt. 'How can you not like them?'

'No, we love them,' I said quickly.

'Yeah, we love them,' Marianne repeated, with not nearly enough enthusiasm.

'It's just,' I said, in the sort of gentle tone that I might use for telling a child that they could no longer go to Disneyland *after* they'd packed their bag and put on their Mickey Mouse ears, 'don't you think it might be a bit tricky to get on them if we're wearing bridesmaid dresses?'

Marianne nodded in agreement but Fenella stepped

forward, always on hand to solve the problem. 'That's why you'll ride side-saddle.'

'Isn't that what they did when Jane Austen was alive?'

'It is still practiced today, Anastasia,' Fenella said. I scowled at the use of my full name – Dad only brought it out when I'd done something seriously wrong. Then she added, 'by those who are *ladylike* of course,' for good measure.

Marianne sniggered for the first time since we arrived, and I scowled.

Whatever. I am totally ladylike, apart from when I'm setting people on fire or crashing into industrial bins while trying to catch a Frisbee (which is what I had done that morning – of course Connor saw me do it, because my life is awful) but those are unique incidents.

'Maybe they're right. Maybe it won't work,' Helena sighed, examining the saddle closely. 'But I do think it would be incredibly elegant.' We all continued to stare at the horses in front of us. The poor groom holding their reins looked like he very much wanted to go home. 'And they are so beautiful.'

That was true. The two horses were magnificent. They were both grey and had beautifully long, glossy manes and tails. I could see why Helena was so attached to them already.

'If Sophie Parker were a horse, she would definitely be one of these,' I observed out loud. 'And I'd be a donkey.'

Marianne rolled her eyes. 'Why do you always have to say the most random things?'

'Helena, you'll never be able to decide unless you see them in action. Remember what I told you, visualisation is so important before making key decisions.' Fenella closed her eyes and took a deep, intense breath, as though she was leading a yoga class. 'Visualise your wedding.' Helena closed her eyes too and, following Fenella's example, dramatically inhaled through her nose. 'Do not let your worries overcome you. See it, feel it, live it. This will be your day.'

Helena nodded, and Marianne and I shared a smirk just before she re-opened her eyes. 'Yes. This is important, girls. Up you hop.'

'Huh?' Marianne jumped a little as one of the horses whinnied loudly.

'Didn't you hear Fenella? I need to see you on the horses before I make a decision.' Helena folded her arms and Fenella, her job done, began scribbling again. 'The groom can help you up. Look, he has little stepladders for you.'

'Mum, I don't think this is a good idea. I haven't been up on a horse in forever.'

'Oh please, Marianne, you were a natural. Side-saddle should be a doddle. Anna, how confident are you on a horse?'

'Well, today I ran for a Frisbee and crashed into some of the school's industrial bins, so considering I'm not brilliant on my own feet, I'm not sure how great I'll be on someone else's hooves.'

'Sorry, what?' Marianne looked baffled. 'You crashed into some bins?'

'Yes, Marianne, industrial bins. I don't want to dwell.'

'Did Connor see?' she asked carefully.

'Yes. Of course he did. While he was talking to Stephanie, a girl with a blunt-cut fringe who enjoys Art and milkshakes. Like I said, Marianne, I do not want to dwell on it.'

'Here we go, then!' The groom brought over a small stepladder and set it up alongside one of the horses. Then he held out his hand for me to take. I gulped. 'It's easy,' he insisted. 'We'll just get you up there for now. Don't worry, you won't be doing anything strenuous.'

With one last glare at Helena to punish her for making me do such a ridiculous thing after a terrible day at school, I wobbled up the ladder and leaned forward to pat the neck of the horse. 'Don't kill me, OK? I'm going to trust you on this one.'

'Just plonk your bottom on, keeping both legs on the ladder. That's it.' I sat down on the saddle gently as the groom continued his instructions. 'Now swing your right leg over that pommel at the front – the sticking-up bit – and your leg will naturally dangle this way. And now your left foot goes in the stirrup, like that. There you go! You are sitting side-saddle!'

I peered down at the others. 'How do I look?' I squeaked.

'Ridiculous,' Marianne said.

'No, she doesn't,' Helena retorted, narrowing her eyes at Marianne.

'Yes, she does.'

'No, she doesn't.'

'Mum, you're being absurd.'

'Why won't you ever give things a try, Marianne?'

'Why do you always insist I try stupid things?'

'I'm only asking you to try side-saddle!'

'That *is* a stupid thing!'

'How do you know if you won't try it?'

'I don't have to try sitting sideways on a horse to know that we would look like utter freaks arriving at your wedding on horses that we can't ride.'

'Well, if you tried, you might find you can!'

'Well, if you –'

'OI!' I yelled, in an attempt to shut them up.

This had the desired effect. But what also happened was that the horse, spooked by my yelling in his ear, lurched forward in a panic. The others gasped, which made the horse even more agitated. I clung on desperately, yelling at the horse to stop, but, like everyone else on the planet these days, he completely ignored me.

By the time the groom managed to catch up and grab the reins, slowing the horse to a walk, I was lying face down on his back, hugging his neck and praying that I didn't fall off. I had done that enough for one day.

Marianne rushed over to steady me as I was helped down. She looked worried. Helena looked resolute.

'You're absolutely right, Fenella, you really do have to see things to make decisions.' She turned to us. 'Horses are a big fat no. Come on, let's go. Thank you, Anna, that was very helpful.'

I wiped the sweat of fear from my brow. 'You're welcome,' I whispered as I was led back to the car.

From: jess.delby@zingmail.co.uk
To: anna_huntley@zingmail.co.uk
Subject: The bins

I can't believe Josie. She only said that to impress Sophie.

She's a coward, don't listen to her.

J x

From: anna_huntley@zingmail.co.uk
To: jess.delby@zingmail.co.uk
Subject: Re: The bins

Actually, I think Josie could have said a lot worse than, 'once a loser, always a loser.' It's not even original; I overheard her saying that about me last term so you don't need to worry.

Anyway, considering that I had just bashed into a load of big green bins and was lying sprawled on the ground, she kind of had a point.

Why do they make me play team games in PE?

Love, me xxx

From: jess.delby@zingmail.co.uk
To: anna_huntley@zingmail.co.uk
Subject: Re: The bins

I guess it would have been a little better if you had actually caught the Frisbee. You missed it by a mile. Maybe they need to introduce horse riding in PE. You'd be *great* at that.

J x

From: anna_huntley@zingmail.co.uk
To: jess.delby@zingmail.co.uk
Subject: Re: The bins

Thanks, Jess, you always make me feel better.

I'm so lucky to have you here to point out these things to me when I feel down.

Love, me xxx

From: jess.delby@zingmail.co.uk
To: anna_huntley@zingmail.co.uk
Subject: Re: The bins

Have you got 'good at sarcasm' down on the list that your mum and Helena came up with?

J x

From: anna_huntley@zingmail.co.uk

To: jess.delby@zingmail.co.uk

Subject: Re: The bins

ARE YOU ALL IN THIS TOGETHER?????

I decided that it was time for an emergency meeting of the gang at my house. So I called over Jess and Danny, gave them ice cream, and then began my announcement.

'No, no, no,' said Jess, shaking her head.

'What?! I haven't even *said* anything yet!'

'Yes you have.'

'I just said, "right, Gang".'

'Precisely.' She shoved the spoon defiantly into her ice cream. 'I refuse to let you call us "Gang". It's really embarrassing, especially since you said it as though it was capitalised. You can get away with a lot of things, but "Gang" is not one of them. You're not that endearing.'

'FINE.'

Danny rolled his eyes at us and tickled Dog's ears. Dog loves it when Jess and Danny came over – he's never short of attention. He can pretty much guarantee he will be fussed over by someone at every single point of the evening.

I was pleased that Dog was getting spoilt – he had

been so neglected by Dad recently. Dad protested that he was paying more than enough attention to him, and I should stop complaining, but he knew the truth really, and so did I.

Since Helena had got a wedding team and her head had become full of owls, macarons and side-saddle, she hadn't been coming round nearly so often. This was traumatic for Dog, as he had really grown fond of her – he'd even stopped taking her designer clutch bags and putting them in his water bowl for safe keeping, a very clear sign of respect. I spoke to Dad about Helena's absence having an impact on Dog but Dad just sighed and said, 'She's . . . busy, Anna. Things are just a little hectic at the moment.' I told him that she'd probably come round more often if he stopped talking about boring things like tanks all the time and he slammed the study door in my face.

Talk about ungrateful.

Dog kept punishing Dad for all the change he was making him suffer – the sitting on the glasses incident was just one example. There had also been an anxiety-inducing moment earlier in the week when Dad thought he had lost his car keys, but it turned out that Dog had eaten them.

'It's because you keep leaving him behind,' I said. 'It's so obvious. Look at the symbolism! He ate your car keys.

He was trying to tell you something. You owe him, Dad.'

'I owe him? I OWE HIM?!' Dad's eyebrows jumped vigorously about on his forehead. 'Do you know how much it cost to have the keys safely removed at the vet's?'

'Dad, it is very unclassy of you to discuss money.'

Dog and I had watched as his face went cherry-red and he stormed out of the room and into his study, slamming the door. Then Dog went back to chewing the corners of all the kitchen cupboards.

So it was good for Dog to have some down time with Danny and Jess, and anyway, he was a key member of the gan– I mean, *team*.

'Right, *friends*, I'm sure you all know why you're here this evening.'

'Anna, why are you talking like a doofus? And do you have to be holding that ruler and pacing around the room?'

'Also,' Danny added, 'where did you get that flipchart?'

'I borrowed it from school, but that's not important.' I propped the chart up on the sofa and flipped over the cover so that we had a blank A3 page staring at us. 'I need your help to come up with a strategy.'

They both stared back at me in confusion.

I had made a conscious decision on the way back from the side-saddle adventure: I needed to find something to be good at. Marianne, my mum and Helena hadn't helped identify any useful talents during their email exchange, so we needed to think outside the box. We need to work out something impressive that I could learn to do, and quickly. And, most importantly, it had to be something that Connor would be impressed by.

'Why are you letting that stupid article get to you? It's the journalists that made you famous when they put you on their covers in the first place. Tanya's just a stupid hypocrite,' Jess pointed out, passing Danny the ice cream and fishing her camera out of her bag.

'Anna, the media can create something out of nothing. What they make you out to be has nothing to do with the real you,' Danny related in a wise, Yoda-like tone.

'It's not just the media. It's everyone else too. What if that sign pinned up on my locker door is right? I'm a loser. It's just like Josie said: "Once a loser, always a loser".' I grumpily got out my marker pen and scribbled LOSER in bold red across the centre of the flipchart page. Jess sighed. 'It doesn't have to be something huge. But next time a journalist tells me that It Girls are a waste of space, I want to be able to argue back. So I need your help.'

'Right then.' Danny rubbed his hands together. 'Let's do this. Let's just write any ideas that pop into our heads.

Anna, you're the scribe, since you have the marker pen: put down anything we yell out.'

'SOMMELIER!' Jess immediately cried, as though she had been bursting to say it for ages.

'Jess, do you know what a sommelier is?' Danny folded his arms pompously.

'It's someone who tastes wine for a living, peabrain. My mum's friend is one. You get to travel a lot and it's super sophisticated.'

I considered it, hoping I was spelling it correctly.

'I don't think that's the best idea. Anna will have to wait a few years until she can start learning that.' Danny rolled his eyes, and I jotted *wait until 18?* underneath *Sommelier*.

'What about gift-wrapping?' Jess offered. 'That's something I've always wanted to be good at. It's an underestimated skill for sure.'

Danny turned to address Dog. 'This is going to be a long night.'

After a bit Danny and I stepped back to study our suggestions so far, and Jess decided that this would be the perfect time to document the evening. She took photographs so often these days that I was beginning to forget that the camera was there.

Ghost stories?

Writing?

Origami?

Pottery?

Sommelier?

Gift wrapping?

Loser

Wait until 18?

Flower arranging?

Painting?

Martial arts?

Marry a footballer?

'What do you think, Anna?' she asked, clicking away. 'Any useful options?'

'I don't think we've exhausted everything yet,' I remarked.

'Martial arts? Try a high kick,' Danny suggested. 'Just kick the air, let's see whether it could be a possibility.'

I performed what I was sure was a perfect high kick.

They both hesitated and Jess put her camera down for a moment. 'I don't think we should go in that direction,' Danny said gently.

'You looked like a goat that had caught its leg in an electric fence,' agreed Jess.

'What?' I looked at Jess, appalled by her comment. 'Why a goat?'

'Can't say,' she shrugged. 'That's just the image that came to me. I'm glad I didn't catch that on camera. Not one for the album.'

'Bring back the focus, guys,' Danny encouraged. We all looked at the diagram.

'I could marry a footballer?' I sat down and put my head in my hands. 'Oh no! Is that really my last option? That's not something you can even be good at!'

'Some people are very good at it,' Jess joked. Danny rolled his eyes and sat down next to me, defeated. Jess slumped into a chair opposite.

'So this confirms it. I'm doomed to be good at nothing for the rest of my life.'

Danny placed a comforting hand on my shoulder and Dog wandered over to rest his head in my lap in sympathy. 'And I'll never be able to marry a footballer, anyway, because I'm not Sophie Parker. I crash into bins and set people on fire! Honestly, I don't even have what it takes to be a trophy wife!'

Jess suddenly sat bolt upright.

'*What* did you just say?' she demanded, her eyes wide with hope.

'Er –'

'You just said *trophy wife*.'

'Yes?' I turned to Danny, but he looked as bewildered as I felt.

'Trophy wife!' Jess cried, waiting for us to get it. '*Trophy*!'

She ripped the 'LOSER' page off the pad and left it scrumpled on the floor. Then she grabbed the marker pen and, in much bigger letters than I had used, scribbled *TROPHY*.

'Jess, you're going to have to enlighten us here.'

'You said you wanted a way to show people that they could look up to you, right?'

'Yeah?'

'Well, what if you were a loser who became a *winner*? Everyone loves those kind of stories!'

'Jess,' Danny ran his hand through his curls, 'what are you *talking* about?'

'How can you guys not have got it yet?' She shook her head. 'How could Anna inspire others? By showing them that by working hard you can achieve anything you set your heart on, even if it seems impossible at first.'

'That would obviously be perfect. But I have no idea what I could set my heart on.'

'I do.' She pointed at *TROPHY* again.

Danny let out a low whistle. 'Do you mean – ?'

'Yes, Danny, I do.'

'How have I still not got this?' I yelled indignantly.

Danny nodded. 'You're right, Jess. It's genius. But can we pull it off?'

'Anna can. It Girls can. That's the point!' Jess grinned at me, folding her arms. 'Anna, you need to put yourself forward as team captain for the Puffins. Then, for the first time in years, you are going to make us win sports day.'

'Wh-what? No way!' I looked at both of them in alarm. 'NO WAY!'

'It's exactly what you wanted!'

'Captain? *Sports day*? I can't! No one will ever want me as their captain, I'm –'

'*A loser*?' Jess leaned in close to my face and waggled her finger in front of my nose. 'No, you're not. You, my friend, are an It Girl. Remember, *you* don't have to be the best athlete – you just have to *inspire* others to be.'

I looked at Danny, waiting for him to laugh in Jess's face.

No such luck.

'It's brilliant, Jess. No one would ever think that Anna could lead the Puffins to victory, but she will. Can you imagine Sophie Parker's face?' Danny beamed at me. 'You'll show everyone that they can be whoever they want to be, no matter what anyone else thinks.'

'And that, Anna Huntley,' Jess concluded, whacking the lid back on the marker pen triumphantly, 'will be your thing.'

You think it's too much?

Jess, Miss Brockley is looking particularly sprightly today. I don't think we should risk note-passing, she's sure to catch us.

She's not looking this way right now. Anyway, I need to know what you think about your new publicity! Do you like it? I got a little overexcited.

I can tell.

Everyone's talking about it, Anna. I think it's GREAT!

I'm aware that they're all talking about it. Walking down the corridor this morning caused quite a stir.

Why aren't you more excited?!

I don't know. Don't you think we should at least have waited until I'd done some training before you put huge posters and banners up ALL OVER THE SCHOOL?

Danny said you'd react like this. You could be a little more grateful. Those posters took me ages.

And they are seriously good, I have to say. Don't get me wrong, you really outdid yourself — you must have literally bought a huge tub of glitter.

It was actually a barrel.

Impressive. You should draw pictures of puffins for a living. You're weirdly good at it.

You are going to be the best Puffin team captain ever! I wish I'd seen Sophie's face when she walked into school this morning and saw the walls covered in ANNA HUNTLEY FOR PUFFIN TEAM CAPTAIN! banners.

She probably laughed her head off.

No way! She's intimidated by you really.

You think that SOPHIE PARKER is intimidated by ME? Are you out of your mind?!

You'd be surprised. You're the It Girl, remember, not her. Have you spoken to the Sports department yet?

Jess, it's the first lesson of the day, I haven't had a chance to. How did you have the time to put all those things up before we arrived? You must have come in seriously early.

Nah, I came in over the weekend.

The school is locked over the weekend.

I broke in.

What?

I broke in.

WHAT?

It's not that hard. Anyway, do you promise you'll go and speak to the Sports department at lunch to nominate yourself?

I promise. Although I still think that this is a bad, bad idea. I don't know why I let you talk me into it.

It is not a bad idea. It's my idea. And I am a genius.

You're a fugitive from the law.

All in a day's work. Here comes Brockers. Over and out, Captain!

When I turned the corner to the Sports department, Sophie was standing outside the door. I considered turning right around and getting out of there, but she spotted me before I had the chance to run the other way. Her mouth curled into a sneer.

'Let me guess why you're lurking around here,' she muttered, careful to keep her voice quiet enough that any teachers in the Sports office wouldn't be able to hear her.

'I imagine for the same reason you are,' I said, a lot more confidently than I felt.

I wish I didn't keep putting myself in situations where I incurred the wrath of the most popular girl in my year. Why couldn't I be like Stephanie? She isn't one of the popular group, but she doesn't get in their way so they never say anything mean to her. I, on the other hand, had already set fire to the Queen Bee's best friend and stole her boyfriend and was now going up against her on my least favourite day of the school year. No wonder she hated me.

'They told me I was a natural choice for the Eagles,' she said smugly.

'Great. Have you knocked?'

'Yes, they're having a meeting. They said they'd be done in a minute.'

I sat down on the bench beside the wall. Sophie remained standing – clearly sitting next to me wasn't an option. She shifted from foot to foot, fiddling every so often with her short skirt and twirling the ends of her hair. After a while the silence got to her. 'Why are you doing this? Seriously,' she huffed, putting her hands on her hips.

'Putting myself forward to captain the Puffins?' I asked nervously.

'Duh.'

I shrugged. 'I want to prove to myself that I can do it.'

'But you hate sport. And you're awful at it. Like, terrible.'

'I would agree with you.'

'I thought I was going to die of laughter when you crashed into the bins the other day in PE. I mean, who does that? It's like you have some kind of problem.'

'Those bins shouldn't be next to a sports pitch. They're a health and safety hazard.'

She snorted. 'The Puffins are going to lose, they always do. I don't get it, Anna, it's like you go out of your way to embarrass yourself.' She shook her head at me like I was the stupidest person in the world.

Thankfully the department door swung open before Sophie could pile any more abuse on me, and Miss Clifford, the head of Sports, stepped out. She acknowledged Sophie with a curt nod, but a large smile spread across her face when she clocked me on the bench. 'So,' she began, 'those posters weren't a joke, then?'

'Unfortunately not.'

'I'm pleased to hear it. Sophie, I take it you're here to put yourself forward for team captain of the Eagles?'

'Yes, Miss Clifford,' Sophie smiled with a sickeningly innocent expression. 'I believe I can lead the Eagles to victory once again. You know how hard I work and how passionate I am about sports.'

'Yes, thank you, Sophie.' Miss Clifford waved her hand. 'You can go now.'

Sophie looked slightly taken aback at being so promptly dismissed, but quickly recovered herself. She gave me one last scowl before whipping out her phone and tottering back towards the main building. Down the hallway I saw Josie, Brendan and James Tyndale waiting for her. When they saw me, Brendan smirked and nudged James, who gave Brendan a semi-joking shove back in return. They clearly all thought my selection would mean an automatic win for the Eagles team.

Miss Clifford watched them go and then sat down on the bench next to me. 'I don't need to tell you, Anna, that most people will be a little surprised at you nominating yourself.'

'If you want to say no now, that is absolutely fine with me,' I said, standing up. I was secretly thrilled at the thought that I might not be allowed to go through with our plan. Jess couldn't be angry at me if the Sports department actually turned me away.

'Wait, I'm not saying no,' she said carefully. 'But I want

to know why. You have no obvious inclination towards sport or athletics. It seems like an odd decision . . . May I ask why you made it?'

'To lead the Puffins to victory,' I said firmly. She seemed unconvinced. 'And,' I sighed, 'to prove that I can?'

Miss Clifford nodded. 'Very well, thank you, Anna. The notice will go up by the end of today.'

I thanked her and then actually ran away. Just being in the Sports department, surrounded by that smell of plastic gym mats and chlorine, made me feel very panicky.

Which was probably not a good thing, considering what I had just put myself forward for.

SPORTS DAY CAPTAINS ANNOUNCEMENT

We are pleased to announce the following two team captains will lead their individual teams at sports day this year:

THE EAGLES
SOPHIE PARKER

THE PUFFINS
ANNA HUNTLEY

Congratulations and good luck!

I hit Josie Graham in the face with a discus.

It wasn't entirely my fault. She should have been standing way further back than she was. OK, yes, it was technically me who released the discus a bit later than you're supposed to, and sure, no one was expecting that I would be so sportingly challenged that I would release a discus in the exact opposite direction of where it was meant to be thrown.

If you think about it, though, Josie was lucky that it was me throwing it and not someone with actual ability, otherwise it might have caused her a lot more damage than a bleeding nose. She might have broken it. She should be GRATEFUL.

Then again, someone with ability probably wouldn't have thrown it backwards.

Still.

We watched Josie being led to the nurse by one of Sophie's other simpering minions, Debbie. Jess, of course, found the whole thing hilarious. 'Right in her face,' she wheezed, in between shrieks of laughter.

'It is NOT funny!' I hissed.

My view was very much shared by Sophie herself, who came storming over towards us, face like thunder.

'Uh oh,' I whimpered, fully aware that everyone was watching and waiting for the fireworks.

'How DARE you hit Josie in the face with a discus?!'

'It was an accident!'

'HA!'

'Sophie, I –'

'Miss Clifford! Miss Clifford!' she cried shrilly, pointing at me furiously. 'You saw the whole thing! It was sabotage!'

'Sabotage?' Jess rolled her eyes. 'That is so stupid.'

'She did it on purpose!'

'Now gir–' Miss Clifford tried to interject.

'Anna's just terrible at discus, Sophie,' Jess corrected her. 'Don't try and twist it. We all know Josie was standing close to the line so she could make fun of Anna. If anyone is trying to sabotage sports day, it's the Eagles.'

'Don't try and twist this round.' Sophie squared up to Jess. 'It's not a Puffin who's been led crying and bleeding to the school nurse today. Josie might not recover by sports day and she's one of the best members of our team!'

'She has a nose bleed,' Jess snorted, 'I have an inkling she might make it to sports day in six weeks' time.'

'See, Miss Clifford? Not an inch of sympathy or remorse for the pain Anna's caused my best friend.'

'Sophie, I think that's a bit muc–' Miss Clifford tried again.

'I have remorse,' I squeaked, but I was ignored too.

'Sounds to me like you're very worried about sports day, Sophie,' Jess observed, folding her arms smugly. 'Feeling threatened by the Puffins, are we? You should be.'

Sophie's jaw dropped open. 'You have got to be kidding,' she snapped. 'The Puffins don't have a chance of winning. Especially when their team captain is a complete LOSER who hits people in the face with sports equipment.'

'Hey!' I protested.

'Technically, she's right,' Jess said with a wink at me before putting her hands on her hips to mimic Sophie's I-am-superior-to-everyone-here stance. 'Sophie, this year the Puffins are going to win. I would much rather have a loser who hits people in the face with sports equipment as our team captain than a whining princess like you.'

'Girls!' Miss Clifford finally managed to make herself heard over Sophie and Jess's bickering. 'I don't want another word out of either of you. Sophie, go to the school nurse and check that Josie is OK.'

'But –'

'Now, Miss Parker.' Miss Clifford stood firm. Sophie clenched her fists and furiously spun round. She stomped across the pitch, her long ponytail swishing dramatically from side to side, and the rest of the class moved very quickly to get out of her way. 'And Jessica, I don't want you to talk like that in my lesson again, is that clear?'

'Miss Clifford, she was accusing –'

'I don't care what she was doing,' she said sternly. 'No more fighting.'

Jess looked down at her trainers.

'Right,' Miss Clifford announced to the rest of the class. 'Let's move on to another activity, shall we?'

Everyone started talking, moving in a huddle towards the long jump. 'Oh, and Anna?' Miss Clifford stopped me with a smile as I followed the crowd. 'Try not to kill anyone before sports day, would you?'

That evening, the doorbell rang and Dad answered. He yelled up to say that it was for me and disturbed my re-enactment of a scene from a John Wayne Western with Dog (he always plays an excellent bartender – he sits there and looks confused, which is perfectly in character). I thought it might be Connor standing outside my house. In fact, I really hoped it was.

I hadn't seen him properly since the press conference,

unless you count catching a glimpse of him while I lay sprawled on the floor after I'd crashed into those bins, and I'd been so mortified then that I'd got up and run in the opposite direction.

But now that I had gained my own thing (a team captain thing!) to be proud of, a thing that would show everyone how wrong the media was about me being a typical It Girl, I'd hardly seen him around at all.

I didn't blame him. I would have been embarrassed by me too. But as I approached the door, remembering at the last minute to take my cowboy hat off and leave it on the telephone table, I couldn't stop the butterflies in my stomach going off at the thought of seeing him again.

'James is here to see you,' Dad informed me with raised eyebrows as he walked past me to the sitting room

Huh?

I peered round the door to see James Tyndale on my step. *James Tyndale*? Why was JAMES TYNDALE at my house?

'Hello?'

'Hey Anna,' he said brightly, then his expression turned to confusion. 'Is that a toy pistol?' He pointed at my jeans pocket.

'Oh.' I took it out. 'Yeah. I've been watching some Western movies. You know.'

'Right,' he said, looking a little freaked out.

I quickly threw the pistol over my shoulder. I heard a yelp and spun round to see Dad rubbing his head by the sitting room door. He'd clearly been standing there eavesdropping. '*Go away*!' I mouthed and he slunk off, no doubt with the full intention of lingering behind the door to do exactly the same again.

'Sorry,' I turned back to James, 'do you mind me asking what you're doing here? Are you here to yell at me about Josie? Didn't she get all those flowers I sent?'

'I'm not here about Josie. I asked Jess for your address.' He took a deep breath. 'I'm, er, here for you.'

'I'm sorry?'

'Well, for the Puffins to be more exact. I want us to win this year.'

'OK. I'll do my best. Thanks for coming round. I'll see you in school.'

'I mean it, Anna. The Eagles win every year and Brendan never lets me forget about it. This year I want to be on the winning team, and you're the key to that. I'm here to offer my services as your personal trainer.'

'HA!' I snorted through my nose. Trust me, I wish I'd had a more dignified response, but either James was taking the mick or he'd recently had a knock on the head.

Why I was sure James Tyndale must have suffered a recent knock on the head:

1. James Tyndale was one of the most popular boys in our year.

2. James Tyndale was friends with Brendan, a boy who I did not have the best history with.

3. James Tyndale had never spoken to me before.

4. Except maybe once last term, while I was sort of friends with the popular group.

5. I can't really remember, though, so I don't think it counts.

6. He had just offered me, ANNA HUNTLEY, the worst sportswoman OF ALL TIME, personal training lessons.

'Why are you doing that with your face?' asked James.

'I'm not doing anything with my face.' What was I doing with my face? Why couldn't I exercise control over my own face? 'I just don't understand why you're doing this.'

He looked uncomfortable. 'Well, I'm good at athletics and you're rubbish. So I'm going to train you up so we can win on sports day. That's it . . . really.'

'*Really*? Can I ask you something?'

'Shoot.'

'Why do you care so much about sports day?'

He narrowed his eyes. 'Why do *you* care so much? You're not who I imagined might put themselves forward to be captain.'

'Ah,' I sighed and bit my lip. 'It's a long story but it's about . . . proving something.'

'Same,' said James.

'What on earth could you possibly have to prove?!'

'That I can be the best at something.'

'HA!'

'I don't know why you're laughing,' he said, crestfallen. 'I'm serious. Look, Brendan is my best friend. But he also happens to be the best at everything. Looks, sports, grades. I come second at everything.'

'Better than coming last. That happens to me all the time.'

He raised an eyebrow. 'Seriously. This time I want to come first for a change. Sounds lame,' he shrugged, 'but I don't care.'

I stared at him. He stared right back.

'You're being serious.'

'Yes.'

'You're not playing a big joke on me.'

'No.'

'You want to train me up?'

'Yes.'

'You're not giving very enthusiastic or detailed answers.'

'You're not asking very enthusiastic or detailed questions.'

'Look, James, I need to tell you now that I don't have any strengths that we can play on. Trust me, I have a list and none of them are useful at all unless I plan on entering an animal impersonation competition.'

'OK, that's weird, but I'm not going to ask,' he said. 'But I think you do have a strength, actually.'

'I do?'

'You're nice.'

I paused and then burst out laughing.

'I mean it. I think we can use that.'

'I honestly have no idea what you're talking about.'

'I was going to put myself forward for captain. But after I saw all the posters – they are VERY glittery by the way – and then I saw you sitting with Miss Clifford, I realised something important. No one is scared of you. There's a stupid video of you on the Internet in a plant pot, and that makes you approachable. You're the best person in the school to motivate and encourage the Puffins. You just need some – well, quite a lot of – help.'

'That is EXACTLY what Jess said at the beginning of term. Did she put you up to this? Where is she hiding?' I peered down the road. 'How is she so stealthy? I think it's because she's lean.'

He ignored me. 'Great. We'll start tomorrow after school. I'm obviously going to need full commitment on your part: fitness levels, practice, eating healthily. I can map it all out for you.'

'Are you being *serious*? Tomorrow is the start of half term. I'm on holiday!'

'Don't I look serious? Anna, if you really want to be team captain, you're going to have to compete in four events including the final relay. If you don't think you can do it then you should stand down.'

I thought about that. I thought about not having seen Connor for so long, and liking him so much. And I thought about what I wanted him – and everyone else – to think of me and all that fame that had unintentionally come my way.

'FINE,' I huffed. 'But don't expect me to wear any lycra.'

'Great,' he grinned. 'Make sure you have sports gear on tomorrow. Don't forget your trainers!' And he turned and jogged back down the road. Did that boy never stop exercising? Who *jogged* everywhere?

'Anna Huntley,' I turned round to see my dad emerging from the sitting room and slowly shaking his head, a grin spreading across his face, 'what on earth have you got yourself into?'

I quickly realised that James Tyndale was A PSYCHO WHO WAS TRYING TO KILL ME.

Firstly, he made fun of my sportswear. And not even in a cute, cheeky way, like Connor would, but in a blunt, grumpy way that I didn't like at all.

'No, go and change.'

'What? You said sports stuff!'

'Yeah, sports stuff, Anna,' he said, looking down the road as though he was bored already. 'Denim shorts do not count as sportswear.'

'I can run in these. I checked. Dog and I did laps of the house earlier.'

'Just put on your school kit.'

'No!' I stropped. 'What happens if I get photographed? You never know who might be lurking in the bushes.'

'Hurry up, Anna,' he said, looking at his watch. 'There's a game on later that I don't want to miss.'

I changed, and we ran (RAN!) all the way to the park. A few metres down the road I stopped to have a well-deserved breather but James – completely ignoring my human rights – pulled me forward by the arm and forced me to keep going.

'JAMES!' I cried, clutching my side. 'We have to stop! I'm DYING.'

'You're not dying, it's just a stitch. Come on, we've not even reached the end of your road!'

OK, you know what, James? It's a really long road.

By the time the railings of the park loomed into view I was practically crawling and threw myself heroically towards them, clinging on tightly as I slid down slowly into a heap on the pavement.

'Right,' said James, who didn't appear to have even broken a sweat. 'Let's warm up.'

SORRY?!

'We just ran all that way!' I wheezed. 'I thought that was our session done!'

'No,' he snorted, looking mightily unimpressed as I cuddled the railings tighter and struggled to get my breath back, 'that was just us getting to the park. Your session begins now.'

The second session was even worse. This time he ran – WHAT WAS THE RUSH? – right into my house without being invited. 'You have a dog, don't you?' he asked. 'You brought him along once when you were hanging out with Brendan. Unless you know a person called Dog. Which is almost as stupid as having a dog named Dog.'

'After a comment like that, I don't think you deserve to meet him again,' I announced loftily, hoping that this rudeness might get me out of another exercise/torture session.

Unfortunately Dog, having heard his name, came bounding into the hall, looking for a new admirer (Dad was still being neglectful). He launched himself at James, licking his face all over. I thought James might be upset, but instead he started to laugh.

I sighed as Dog began chasing his tail in excitement and James grabbed his lead from its hook next to the door. 'You are a traitor and a man trollop, Dog.'

Reasons why you should never exercise with Mr Dog Huntley:

1. He has a tendency to let his tongue droop out of his mouth as he runs next to you.

2. His tongue has slobber on it.

3. This slobber sprays all over your legs.

4. Every time he sees something that might be a squirrel he pounces, almost breaking the arm that is attached to his lead.

5. When he realises that it's only a chocolate wrapper blowing in the wind, and not a squirrel, he stops suddenly and tries to eat it.

6. But when you stop to tie your shoelace, he headbutts you.

7. When evil James Tyndale pulls a tennis ball out of his pocket and throws it, Dog doesn't hesitate to chase it.

8. This means that you are jerked forward before you have time to let go of his lead.

9. Then you fall on to the ground and lie with your face in the dust.

10. You wonder what you've done to James Tyndale to make him want to kill you.

'Anna!' James scolded as I attempted to pick myself up from the ground. My limbs were so weary from all the running, though, that it was taking twice the time it normally would. 'You were meant to try to keep up with Dog!'

'Keep. Up. With. Dog?' I puffed, leaning forward with my chin held up so that I could glare at James while I caught my breath. 'You don't know what he's capable of.'

'I said "try to". You didn't even try. You need to train mentally as well, you know.' He tapped the side of my head. 'Now, ten sit-ups as punishment for not even trying to run with your dog. Look, he's coming back now. He looks *ashamed* of you.'

Actually, Dog didn't look ashamed at all. He looked extremely happy, the tennis ball firmly in his jaw and his long pink tongue lolling out of the side of his mouth.

I gritted my teeth and reminded myself exactly why I was doing this. I was going to be an inspirational team captain and ensure that I would no longer be famous for no reason.

That did not, however, stop me making pointed comments about control freaks in the direction of my so-called trainer (or, more likely, secret MI5 assassin) as I got down and started doing sit-ups. James held my feet on the ground and yelled in my face every time I came up into the sitting position.

'Five more! Come on, put some effort into it.'

'I. Hate. This.' I strained, my whole body aching as I pulled myself up on each word.

I finally collapsed back on to the ground, and Dog decided to drop his slobbery tennis ball right on my mouth. 'BLEUGH!' I cried, wiping my mouth with my arm, grabbing the tennis ball and lobbing it away from me for Dog to fetch.

'Ready for more?' James laughed.

'Go. Away.'

From: jess.delby@zingmail.co.uk
To: anna_huntley@zingmail.co.uk
Subject: Where are you??

I just called again, but your dad keeps saying that you're out on a run.

You know, you should tell him that if he's going to lie, he should really come up with realistic excuses.

Also he got really grumpy with me because I've called twice this morning.

J x

From: anna_huntley@zingmail.co.uk
To: jess.delby@zingmail.co.uk
Subject: Re: Where are you??

Hey! I would call you back, but I think Dog has put the phone somewhere. I can't find it and he's looking very smug about something.

I *was* out on a run. With James Tyndale. It's a long story.

But now I'm back and Dog and I are watching a movie.
We're staying out of Dad's way because he's being grumpy.

Helena wants him to pick out a pattern for the wedding
napkins – she's given him a booklet with the history and
meanings of each pattern – but he's also on deadline for
the chapter he's working on, so he's stressing out.

I did suggest that she comes round and just picks one to
put him out of his misery but apparently she's too busy. As
usual.

I tried to help. I poured Dad a drink, because he was pacing
around his study yelling and complaining, but when I went
in with it just now, he sniffed it and then yelled, 'Cointreau?
ARE YOU MAD?'

Rude.

Love, me xxx

From: jess.delby@zingmail.co.uk
To: anna_huntley@zingmail.co.uk
Subject: Re: Where are you??

You were actually on a RUN? OK, tell me what is going on immediately.

Also, we've been through this. Dog is a DOG and therefore cannot have facial expressions.

Why did you pour your dad Cointreau? That's a very random selection.

J x

From: anna_huntley@zingmail.co.uk
To: jess.delby@zingmail.co.uk
Subject: Re: Where are you??

To be honest, I have no idea why I picked that bottle. I just went with my gut. My gut said Cointreau.

I will never go with my gut again.

I'm telling you, Dog looks smug. I bet you he's put the phone in the bin again. It's like a dog version of basketball for him. He kind of slam-dunks it in. I shouldn't have encouraged that game.

James is training me up for sports day, to make sure I don't come last in everything. Didn't he explain that when he asked for my address?

Love, me xxx

From: jess.delby@zingmail.co.uk
To: anna_huntley@zingmail.co.uk
Subject: It all becomes clear

He was actually pretty mysterious about the whole thing but that's random/brilliant news!

James is so sporty, he's the perfect person to get help from about that kind of thing.

Plus, you know, you can watch him running about. In his shorts. Nice.

J x

From: anna_huntley@zingmail.co.uk
To: jess.delby@zingmail.co.uk
Subject: Re: It all becomes clear

Stop that talk, you sound like Mum when she's watching Wimbledon.

Hang on a second. You just gave my address to James without asking why he wanted it? He might have been coming over to throw things at me as revenge for me hitting Josie in the face with a discus!

Heck, what were you thinking?!

Love, me xxx

From: jess.delby@zingmail.co.uk
To: anna_huntley@zingmail.co.uk
Subject: ???

Um. Sorry. What? Why did you just write HECK?

Explain yourself at once.

J x

From: anna_huntley@zingmail.co.uk
To: jess.delby@zingmail.co.uk
Subject: Re: ???

What's wrong with heck? It's an everyday word.

Love, me xxx

From: jess.delby@zingmail.co.uk
To: anna_huntley@zingmail.co.uk
Subject: Re: ???

Anna, can I ask you something?

Is there a teeny-weeny chance that the movie you and Dog are currently watching stars John Wayne?

J x

From: anna_huntley@zingmail.co.uk
To: jess.delby@zingmail.co.uk
Subject: Wow.

OK, that's just creepy. HOW DID YOU DO THAT?

Love, me xxx

From: jess.delby@zingmail.co.uk
To: anna_huntley@zingmail.co.uk

Subject: Re: Wow.

You are an open book and I am a genius.

J x

From: anna_huntley@zingmail.co.uk
To: jess.delby@zingmail.co.uk
Subject: Re: Wow.

Oh yeah? Well, if you're so clever, tell me what I'm eating right at this moment.

Love, me xxx

From: jess.delby@zingmail.co.uk
To: anna_huntley@zingmail.co.uk
Subject: Re: Wow.

Nutella. Out of the jar. With a spoon.

Which is naughty. You shouldn't eat Nutella when you're training. You should be having a nice healthy smoothie or something. Put the jar down.

J x

From: anna_huntley@zingmail.co.uk
To: jess.delby@zingmail.co.uk
Subject: Re: Wow.

OH MY GOD, WHERE ARE YOU?!

Hi! You've reached Jess. Leave me a message and I'll give you a buzz.

BEEP

'Ha! I knew you wouldn't pick up. I've foiled your plan, haven't I! Well, Jessica, I'm on to you. You should know that I am currently scouring the sitting room for the hidden camera that you've planted. There is no way you could just GUESS that I was watching a John Wayne movie and eating Nutella. I will discover your device. You can bet on it. Good day to you, young lady!'

Hi! You've reached Jess. Leave me a message and I'll give you a buzz.

BEEP

'So I just rang your home phone. Your mum said you were having a bath. A likely story! You don't want to talk because you can't handle the truth! Tell me where the camera is!'

Hi! You've reached Jess. Leave me a message and I'll give you a buzz.

BEEP

'Buddy, can you give me a clue? Like, could you tell me roughly which area of the room it's in?'

Hi! You've reached Jess. Leave me a message and I'll give you a buzz.

BEEP

'I FOUND IT! Neatly hidden in the clock on our mantelpiece! AHA! You thought you had me fooled, but alas, the truth comes out in the end. Today I, Anna Huntley, am victorious . . . what, Dad? No, I'm on the phone to Jess. No, it's her answerphone. No, I won't hang up. I need to bathe in my glory! What? No, Dad, it's a camera. In the clock! Yes, look, here. What do you mean, it's a cog? It is not a *cog*! It is clearly a camera that spies on people! Dad, I think I know the difference between a spy camera and a simple cog. Hello, you can get them on eBay. Dad, give me that back! It's evidence! Dad! I . . . oh . . . Are you sure? Oh. Right. Yeah, no, I see how that . . . um. Jess, I'm going to have to call you back. OK, bye.'

Ten moments in my life when Dad has been so stressed I thought that his eyebrows might jump off his face:

1. That time in Ireland, when I hid the hire car keys in a bush as a joke, and then forgot which bush they were in.

We were in the land of mischievous leprechauns! Dad really should have remained calm.

2. That time in France when I hid all his euros in the washing machine as a joke, and then forgot about the joke until after we had done the first laundry wash.

But who puts on a wash without checking if there's anything in the washing drum first? I still think it was unfair that Dad yelled at me for so long and kept bringing it up whenever he paid for anything for the rest of the holiday (this was everything as I was a child and he had refused to give me pocket money).

3. That time in Cornwall when I threw out all of the clothes in the wardrobe of the room I was staying

in because I thought a previous guest had left them there. Then it turned out that we were staying in Dad's friend's holiday home.

There's a lesson to be learnt here: be honest with your children! I don't remember Dad mentioning once that it was someone else's house. Which was pretty stupid of him if you ask me – but then, no one ever does.

4. That time, just before Royal Ascot, when I gave Dad's Royal Enclosure ticket and badge to Dog to hold as a joke and he ate them.

His company managed to sort out a replacement before he even arrived, so I don't know what the big deal was.

5. That time I heckled him at one of his yawn book lectures. Mwahahahahahahaha!

6. That time I asked his editor whether he had been on drugs when he made a two-book offer for books on tanks and war weapons by Nicholas Huntley.

Most people would have seen the funny side of this. Dad should really warn me when people with no sense of humour are coming to the house. Then again, I should have guessed about the lack of humour, considering the kinds of book this guy edits.

7. That time Mum came to stay and gave Dad's

keyboard away to a homeless person while he was at work.

I was totally on Mum's side for that one. Dad was rubbish at the keyboard. It had to go.

8. That time Mum came to stay when I was really little, before we had Dog, and Mum bought a pig and let it loose in the house.

Poor Mitch the Pig. Dad never even gave him a chance. Although it would have been easier to persuade Dad to keep him if he hadn't snacked on Dad's books.

9. That time I mixed a whole jar of chilli powder into the Bolognese because I was experimenting and I forgot to tell Dad before he shoved a whole spoonful in his mouth.

Maybe SOME people shouldn't have lazily forced their young daughter to stir the Bolognese for them while they took a phone call.

10. That time when Helena informed him that she'd hired a circus for their wedding.

No comment.

Normally I wouldn't really rate my mum's calming skills, but she's really upped her game lately. When I came back from a gruelling hour-long session with James in which he made me do SPRINTS and SIT-UPS in the park (seriously, why would people do exercise for fun?) Dad was lying on the sofa, and Mum, who was back from her travels for half term as usual, was fanning him with a newspaper.

'Hi Mum, nice to have you here,' I said, looking at Dad warily. 'Is everything OK?'

'Yes, darling, your father's just having a moment. How are you? You look terrible!'

'Thanks, Mum. I've been doing athletics.'

'Anna, what have I told you about lying?'

Why did everyone assume I was lying when I told them I'd been for a run?! But I was too tired to protest. 'What's going on?'

Dad murmured something unintelligible without opening his eyes.

'Mum, why is Dad being weird?'

'Helena has hired a circus for the wedding,' Mum said matter-of-factly. There was a low, pained groan from my father.

'Helena's done what?! Uh oh, maybe that's going too far,' I said.

'She has ABSOLUTELY gone too far!' Dad exploded, leaping up from the sofa and storming across the room.

'Nick!' Mum warned. 'Your blood pressure. You must keep calm.'

'KEEP CALM?!' Dad cried, his eyebrows leaping about twenty feet in the air. 'My fiancée has lost her mind and booked a *circus* for our wedding – which we haven't even got a venue for yet, because she keeps changing her blooming mind!'

Dad paced around the sitting room and Mum and I shared a look. 'Helena's gone from bad to worse, Rebecca, there's no stopping her.' He threw up his hands in exasperation.

'Nicholas, I understand that you're stressed, but if you just talked to her –'

'She won't listen! She won't listen for a second, she's become impossible. Do you know what she had Anna doing the other day? Tell her, Anna, tell your mother what Helena had you doing.'

They both looked at me expectantly. 'She wanted Marianne and me to try riding side-saddle.' Mum blinked at me. 'So we could arrive at the church on horses.'

'SIDE-SADDLE, REBECCA!'

'I heard her, thank you, Nick.'

'Do you know what I had in my house recently? Do you? Do you know?' He marched over to the drinks cupboard and began to pour himself a whiskey. 'Owls. You know, the birds of prey. OWLS. Just flying round my house, willy-nilly.'

'Dad, you can't say willy-nilly. That hasn't been used since the 1800s. True story.'

'OWLS. FLYING AROUND.'

Mum nodded sympathetically.

'I'm sure that if you sit Helena down and have a good long chat with her, you can come to some kind of compromise about the wedding. So that you both get what you want, more or less.'

'Rebecca, I now know the history of about sixteen different napkin patterns. I can reel them off to you now, if you'd like?'

'That's not necessary.'

'Well, if you ever do want to know about napkin patterns, I'm your guy.' Dad collapsed back on to the sofa and shook his head. 'I didn't think it would be this hard.'

'Marriage is very hard,' Mum said gently.

I snorted. 'Like *you* know.'

'Thank you, Anna,' Mum said in that really stern parent voice that immediately makes you want to look down at the floor even if you are completely innocent.

'I wasn't just talking about the wedding.' Dad pushed his hair back and looked across the room at me. 'It's the media attention too. Look at what they're doing to Anna.'

'She does look unnaturally sweaty.'

'I don't mean *literally*, Rebecca. They're victimising her.'

'To be fair, Dad, I did kind of bring it on myself,' I admitted, clicking my fingers for Dog to come and sit by me. Obviously shocked by Dad's mood, he had been anxiously gnawing on the television remote. When he came over I took it from his mouth and offered him Dad's atlas to chew on as a replacement. 'Not every It Girl falls into a plant pot. Or hits people in the face with a discus. Not every It Girl has no real talents.'

'Since my engagement to Helena we've all been caught up in a mad media circus.' Dad rolled his eyes and took another large gulp of whiskey. 'And now she's gone and got an ACTUAL circus!'

'Dad, Mum's right, you should just talk to her. I'm sure she'd be reasonable . . .' I trailed off as he shook his head vigorously.

'She's *completely* unreasonable.' Dad sat back down on the sofa. Mum pulled the newspaper out and began to fan him again.

'I love the woman, but someone needs to talk to her. If this continues,' he said, exhausted, 'there might not even *be* a wedding.'

'Are these shoes really mandatory?' I asked a few days later, as I battled with a pair of very old, very ratty laces.

'Yes! Haven't you ever been bowling before?' Jess laughed, pointing her foot in a ballet-dancer pose. 'I think they're rather fetching.'

'Trust you to be able to pull them off. I look like a clown.'

It had been Danny's idea to go bowling as a break from half term revision. To be honest, I would have agreed to any activity just to get out of the house. Dad had calmed down a little now that Mum had stocked up with plenty of crisps and chocolate so that he could feed himself while he worked on the book, but he was still very tense. He barely spoke to me during the days, which he spent locked away in his study. It made the house quiet for my revision, but I felt just as on edge as Dog.

'I'm weirdly good at bowling,' Danny claimed. He began doing stretches, just like the ones James had been forcing me to do.

'I'll believe that when I see it,' Jess scoffed. 'Hey, Anna, we never considered that bowling might be one of the things you could be good at.'

'I can assure you now that it's not.' I tightened my laces and stood up, ready to go. 'But who knows? Now that I've started training, I might miraculously become good at all sports.'

'How is all of that going?'

'It's . . .' I hesitated. 'It's OK. It's only been a few days but I do think I'm improving, even though James is totally crazy. We're just running at the moment, but when we're back at school he's said that we're going to move on to field events.'

'Ooh, I want to come see this. But I also want to keep all my teeth, so if you could let me know in advance when the discus training begins I'll make sure to be busy those lunchtimes.' Jess clapped me on the back. 'Right, we're ready, let's get going.'

'No, wait,' Danny said, looking at the entrance.

'Why? Our lane is all ready to go.'

'I invited some other people,' he said sheepishly. 'Er, I hope you don't mind.'

'What? Who did you invite?' Jess asked, hands on hips.

'Here they are!' Danny waved, as two very familiar figures came through the doors.

*

'You've got to be joking,' I whispered to Jess in horror.

Stephanie came bounding over, giving us a big wave as she did so. Connor followed close behind her. 'This is SUCH a great idea!' she smiled, beaming at Danny. His cheeks went pink at her attention. 'I've been looking forward to it all day. How's everyone's revision going?'

'Not too bad,' Danny answered. 'Though I'm finding it hard to concentrate sometimes.'

'Me too,' Stephanie agreed. 'It's good to have a break. I thought my brain might explode!'

Danny and Connor agreed. I stayed silent.

'How are you, Anna?' Stephanie asked suddenly, looking very sincere. 'It must be so hard for you, with so much extra pressure – the wedding, I mean, and your social engagements. Let me know if we can do anything to help.'

DANG IT. Why did she have to be so nice?

'Thank you, that's kind of you,' I gritted out.

'Shall we start bowling?' Connor prompted. 'Stephanie and I can get our shoes if you guys want to go get things rolling. No pun intended.'

Stephanie and I both laughed loudly. Jess raised her eyebrows at me and then linked her arm through mine as Danny led the way over to our lane. 'Do you think they're on a date?' I whispered.

'No, they're just friends,' she insisted. 'Anyway, if you're worried, why don't you talk about your training sessions with James Tyndale?'

'You think he'd be impressed that I'm working really hard at being team captain?'

'Maybe,' she shrugged with an impish grin. 'And maybe he'll be a little jealous that James has been spending so much time with you.'

I glanced back to see Stephanie and Connor coming over to join us. 'Do you think so?' I asked desperately.

'Of course!' Jess laughed. 'Don't you know anything about boys?'

Uh, no?

'Hey, Anna, how've you been?' Connor asked, when Jess had skipped over to join Danny, pulling Stephanie along with her. 'Haven't seen you around much.'

I looked at him, sadly remembering how much we used to hang out before Stephanie and her stupid block fringe warped his brain.

'Yeah, I know. You've been spending a lot of time on your Art project.'

'I have. It's very important to me,' he nodded.

'Great.' I smiled weakly. Spending time with Stephanie and his Art project was *important* to him. I felt sick.

'I saw from the pictures that you and Marianne

went to that . . . perfume launch?'

'Yeah, we did. Being an It Girl does have its advantages.' I attempted a small laugh. 'We still get fun invitations, even if we're completely hopeless.'

'You really think –'

Danny got a strike. The cheering from our group distracted Connor from whatever he was about to say. I was quite pleased at the interruption. Things felt awkward between Connor and me. He was probably about to say something like, 'You really think that going to perfume launches is a cool thing to do?'

I bet Stephanie didn't even own perfume. She probably just naturally smelled great.

As I was trying to work out whether it would be socially acceptable to lean over and smell Stephanie, Jess stepped up to the mark and knocked down a few of the pins. 'You're doing it all wrong,' Danny scolded. He turned to Stephanie and me and said, very seriously, 'There's a real skill to bowling, you know.'

Stephanie said, 'Ah,' and nodded admiringly. When she was looking the other way I stuck my tongue out at Danny and Jess shot him a warning look as he opened his mouth again. He closed it pronto.

'Your turn, Stephanie,' Connor announced.

'I bet I'll be rubbish. I'm not really a sporty person,'

said Stephanie. 'Unless there's a paintbrush involved, I tend to be useless at everything.'

'I'm the same,' Connor agreed.

'I'm spending time with James Tyndale,' I blurted. Everyone stopped to look at me – apart from Jess, who hid her face behind a bowling ball in what I presumed was a poor attempt to stifle a laugh. 'I mean, I've been training for sports day.' I attempted to recover the situation. 'As team captain of the Puffins, it's my responsibility.'

'I think it's wonderful that you're team captain,' Stephanie gushed. 'It's so nice to have someone who isn't the obvious choice.'

How. Rude.

'Are you a Puffin?' I asked.

'An Eagle, sadly,' she said. 'I wish I was a Puffin.' She glanced over to where Danny was sitting with Connor. Could she have *been* any more obvious about her reason for wanting to be on our team?

Of course, when she stood up to take her turn, she got a strike.

'Nice!' Danny cheered, giving her a high-five.

'Wow, she really is good at everything,' I muttered, as I shuffled up to the lane.

'Why have you been training with James Tyndale?'

I swung round at the sound of Connor's voice, almost

taking him out with the pink bowling ball I'd just picked up. Luckily his reflexes are really quite good.

'He's coaching me, actually,' I said with an air of indifference. 'We've been running together every day. When we're back at school we'll be starting field training as well as track. He's a lifesaver.' I turned and smiled at the group. 'Because of his training, I'm really getting better.' Then I tried to confidently spin the ball in my hands, but I dropped it. It plunked down heavily, narrowly missed my feet and rolled towards Stephanie. She didn't say anything, just picked it up and handed it back to me. Jess put her head in her hands.

Connor frowned and sat back down next to Stephanie. Danny, who was acting very alpha male for some reason, stepped up to try and instruct me on my technique. He refused to let me have the bars up on the sides of the lane and I zoned out, worrying about Connor's reaction. Had he been annoyed at my mention of training with James? Why hadn't he said so? Maybe he *didn't* care. Maybe he wasn't jealous . . . because he had feelings for someone else now.

I swung the ball down the lane. It plopped down unconvincingly and I managed to knock over one pin.

'Looks like all that sports training is really paying off,' Jess sniggered.

'I think it's really dedicated of you to train for sports day, especially when you're revising too. Connor, you should weave the team captain thing into *The Amazing It Girl*,' Stephanie suggested excitedly. 'It could inspire a whole new storyline!'

Despite the noise from the other lanes, the background music and the clatter of the food bar near us, it felt like the bowling alley had suddenly gone silent. Connor froze, Jess lowered her camera in confusion, Danny looked up from the bowling ball in his hand and Stephanie clapped a palm to her mouth. 'Oh no, Connor, I'm sorry,' she whispered.

'What's *The Amazing It Girl*?' Jess asked, a puzzled look on her face.

'She's seen it?' I asked Connor, my heart beating faster than ever before. Why had he told Stephanie about the comic strip he'd created for me? 'I didn't know you were still working on it.'

'Kind of,' Connor mumbled, his cheeks flushing red as he glanced over at Stephanie. 'What I wanted to do with it has changed a bit and I wanted someone else's opinion, to make sure it wasn't rubbish.'

'Why didn't you ask me?' I asked, an ever-so-slight waver in my voice thanks to the lump forming in my throat.

'What are you talking about?' Jess demanded impatiently.

'Nothing,' Connor said. 'It's not important.'

Sensing the change in atmosphere, Danny put his bowling ball down. He announced that he was going to get some drinks, and Stephanie offered to help carry them. The two of them sidled off leaving Jess, Connor and I in uncomfortable silence. 'Well,' Jess croaked, placing her camera back into her bag and moving towards the lane, 'My turn. I'd better go now, before Mr Know-It-All comes back to criticise my bowling action.'

'Anna, I –' Connor began.

'Don't worry, Connor,' I interrupted. 'I get it.'

He opened his mouth to say something, but then Jess got a strike. She burst into a celebratory dance just as Danny and Stephanie returned with drinks and snacks. *The Amazing It Girl* wasn't brought up again.

Jess called that evening.

'You've just spent the afternoon together,' Dad said, grumpily passing the phone to me. 'How can you still have things to talk about?'

I ignored him. This conversation was important. I had to explain about *The Amazing It Girl*.

'Anna,' Jess said firmly after I'd filled her in. 'He said

he only showed it to her because he wanted to make sure that it was the best it could be. Not because he *likes* her! This whole thing is still cute! I can't believe he's doing this for you.'

'He values her opinion more than mine. He *must* like her. Honestly, Jess, all he seems to do is go to Art classes with her. I've barely seen him since we got back to school.'

'It's a busy term,' Jess said, trying to be comforting.

'I don't know,' I sighed, ignoring Dog trotting into the room dragging an electric fan. 'Maybe he's just realised that he doesn't want a girlfriend who hits people in the face with discuses, falls into plant pots and can't even stand up for herself at a press conference. You heard what he said about *The Amazing It Girl:* "it's not important".'

'It clearly *is* important to both of you. I think you should talk to him,' she suggested.

'Talk to him?' I guffawed. 'And say what?'

'I don't know, genius. How you feel?'

'That is the stupidest idea I've ever heard! I can't just tell him how I feel when he might fancy Stephanie! No, I've got to show him. I've got to be the best team captain ever, otherwise he and the rest of the world will continue to believe that I'm a waste of space.'

'Anna, keep in mind that before any of this happened,

Connor already thought you were amazing. That's why he created that comic strip.'

'Well, now Stephanie has come in and clouded his vision with her clever brain, artistic talents and passion for milkshakes. He even told us that it has *changed*. *The Amazing It Girl* is probably HER now. Sports day will clear things up. I need to show him how determined I am. I am not famous for being completely hopeless!'

Jess sighed heavily at the other end of the phone. 'I don't think Connor thinks you're hopeless.'

'Well,' I said, still not believing her. 'Whatever he thinks, everything's about to change. You just wait and see.'

Despite being the bossiest person I had ever met, James was actually quite easy to spend time with when he wasn't yelling 'motivational' things in my ear or making me do endless laps of the sports field. He'd even shared a little bit about himself. His mum and dad were divorced and he had a little sister who he clearly adored and a pet tortoise named, would you believe it, Tortoise. 'Oh my goodness,' I had squealed excitedly when he told me, 'you were so rude about Dog, when you have Tortoise!'

'My sister named him,' he had said dismissively. 'Now, four more laps and make it quick. I'm meeting Brendan for some football in a bit and I don't want him to guess what we're up to just yet. Our storming victory of the Eagles needs to come as a surprise.' I was still realising that winning this sports day meant as much to James as it did to me.

But when he went into shouting mode, our training sessions still felt like torture.

'Terrible!' he bellowed one lunch break once school

had started again. We were on the sports field, and we were finally beginning to work on events.

I buried my head in the sand. Literally.

James had to stomp over and order me to get out of the sandpit. 'I don't know what that was, but it wasn't a long jump,' he said.

He turned to point at Jess who lowered her camera. 'Is it because Jess is watching? You realise on sports day, there will be *lots* of people watching.'

'You know,' I said, brushing sand off my face, 'you don't have to be so rude.'

He rolled his eyes. 'Anna, you have to admit you didn't even *try* to jump there. You sort of . . . hopped into the sand.'

'For what it's worth, I thought it looked quite graceful,' Jess offered.

'Thank you,' I said.

'She's being sarcastic, Anna. You pretty much tripped over your own feet. You were looking down!'

I looked at Jess accusingly. She averted her eyes and started whistling innocently. 'It's hard to concentrate on jumping when there's so much footwork involved!' I argued, squaring up to him. 'I was looking down because I didn't want to step over that white board thingy.'

'Don't concentrate on that,' he said sternly, putting two

strong hands on my shoulders and looking me hard in the eye. 'I've told you this. Forget about your footing, just run and jump, OK?'

I sighed. 'Fine.'

'Again,' James ordered, pointing at the start of the long jump runway. 'Imagine everyone cheering you on, the whole crowd willing you to jump. Come on, you can do it!'

I focused on the sand, ignoring James clapping his hands and Jess holding her camera at the ready. I took off, running as fast as I could down the runway and then leaping with all the energy I had. I landed with a thump in the sand.

'Much better!' James exclaimed, as Jess whooped loudly. 'Much, much better. Well done!' He clapped me on the back as I rubbed the sand off my hands. 'Now, let's think about the other events.'

Although I tried not to give James the pleasure of seeing me grin, I actually felt quite proud of myself.

'Jess,' James said, 'you'll be the third leg of the relay on the big day, so you'll be passing the baton to Anna. Can you join us again tomorrow to practice the baton pass? We'll do some proper relay sessions later, with all four of us, but it would be great to practice with just the two of you.'

'Of course,' Jess said, practically fluttering her eyelashes. 'Anything I can do.'

Then James bent down to rummage through the box he had borrowed from the PE department and pulled out a stack of discuses. Jess instinctively took a step back.

James, apparently oblivious to Jess, handed me a discus. I took it, trying to be confident and remember what he'd told me before about bending my knees and swivelling my body.

'Should I go and make sure the school nurse is on alert?' Jess asked. I straightened up and gave her a death stare.

'Concentrate, Anna,' said James. Jess went silent. I took a deep breath and then threw the discus as hard as I could.

It landed about a metre in front of us.

James shook his head in dismay.

'That was not that bad!' I said.

'My two-year-old cousin has more upper body strength than you.'

'At least it went forward,' I argued.

'You're the only person in the world who would congratulate themselves on making a discus go forward. Now pick it up and try again. Remember, you want to win!'

'Yes, sir,' I huffed. I made a point of how far I had to

stretch to get it, rolling my eyes at a sniggering Jess.

'Right, try again, and this time put some effort in,' he said, when I'd got back into position with discus in hand – as though I hadn't been doing that the first time. 'Jess, don't distract her.'

Jess held up her hands apologetically and then got her camera at the ready again. Clasping the discus nervously, I breathed slowly like James had taught me, and focused on the position of my feet. Then I threw it with as much strength as I could muster. It flew further than the first time.

James grinned. 'Fist bump!'

I clenched my hand and bumped his fist, delighted, and then skipped over to Jess. 'Not bad eh?' I smiled, putting my hands on my hips proudly.

'Not bad at all,' she agreed – but she was watching James as he ran down to collect the discus.

'Eeew! Jess! Stop it! Have some dignity.'

'What?! I should pretend to be bad at sports so I could get some training sessions from him too.' She winked at me and we erupted into giggles as James came back over.

'You're improving,' he commented, when Jess had rushed off to put her camera away and he and I were walking back to the Sports department to hand back the box of equipment. 'You still need to put in a lot of work, but I think that what's holding you back now is mostly psychological.'

'You mean it's all in my head? James, you've seen me do sport. I don't think I'm imagining how bad I am.'

'That's true,' he agreed. 'You are pretty awful. But look at the way you threw today – that and your sprinting are really improving. I think when sports day comes along, you're going to be a lot better than you think you are, unless you let the way you think affect your performance. At the moment you don't think you can do it, and that's a problem.' He jostled the heavy box in his arms.

'I think you've been standing in the sun shouting at me for too long.'

He gave me a disapproving look. 'I'm serious! If we're going to win, we need to find a way of building up your confidence. Not to be cheesy, but you need to believe in yourself.' He looked thoughtful. 'Is there a reason why your confidence is low at the moment?'

'What, you mean, aside from that newspaper article telling the whole world that I'm a terrible role model and a talentless celebrity?'

'Don't read that stuff. Do you have someone who could make you feel better about yourself? Jess or Danny, maybe?'

'There is someone,' I admitted, a little embarrassed.

'But he's not really . . . available.'

'Are you sure? Maybe you should talk to him about it.' He patted me on the shoulder and then walked off to the boys' changing room. I stared after him thoughtfully.

James was right. I needed to talk to Connor, and I needed to do it now. I made a bee-line for the Art room straight after school, and as soon as I walked in I spotted him. He was leaning on his elbows, hunched over his work with his back to me. I took a deep breath and tried to control the wobbly feeling in my legs.

For once Stephanie wasn't with him. Relieved, I tiptoed through the room, trying not to disturb the other Art students, and tapped his shoulder. He almost jumped out of his skin.

'Anna!' he said, quickly snapping shut his Art folder. 'What are you doing here?'

'I wanted to talk to you about something,' I said, trying to look over his shoulder. I wondered if he was writing *The Amazing It Girl*, but it looked like he was filling out some kind of form. I felt a massive rush of sadness. Had he really stopped working on it?

'How can I help, Spidey?' he asked. He grabbed a stool nearby and dragged it over to his. The stool screeched across the floor and we got looks of irritation from several Art students. Connor and I looked at each other and burst out laughing. I felt another pang. I had missed laughing with him.

'You know how I've been training every day for sports day, learning how not to kill anyone with a discus and stuff?'

'You've been training every day with James Tyndale?' he asked, shifting in his seat and frowning.

'Yeah, you've probably forgotten, but I told you at bowling that he'd –'

'Offered to help you with all your events. I remember. I just didn't realise it was every day. I thought it was more . . . a one-off.'

'Nope,' I said as brightly as I could, confused that things suddenly seemed tense again. 'Strange to think of me doing so much sport, right?'

'It is a bit,' he said quietly.

'Anyway, James said that . . . um . . . well, he thinks I'm not quite there mentally yet.'

Connor laughed. 'I think there have been occasions when, yes, I definitely would agree that you weren't there mentally. The goose incident is a classic example.'

I gave him a look. 'It's not that. I don't think my head's in the game. James thinks I'm not confident enough yet.'

'Does he not,' Connor replied drily.

Why did he sound like that? This wasn't going quite how I planned. 'Er, yes, and he wanted me to spend time with people who can make me feel better about myself.'

Oh god. That sounded awful. Why couldn't I talk to boys like a normal person?

But Connor was looking at me intently. 'And that's me?'

'Um, it doesn't have to be. I know you're busy with your new Art project with Stephanie and –'

A grin slowly spread across this face. 'No way! Hey, I've got an idea. Would you like to have an evening off from revision? I've got an idea for something we could do to build your confidence.'

'Absolutely,' I said without hesitation.

'Cool. Let me pack my stuff away and we can go.'

He sprang to his feet and started shoving everything in his backpack. My heart did backflips. Connor was blowing off an evening of working on his Art project to help me! Did that mean there was a glimmer of hope after all?

'Where are we going?'

'Your house.'

'My house?'

'Yeah, I spotted something on your shelf once when I was round.'

'Spotted what?'

171

'Just come on! We need to get popcorn on the way.'

Popcorn? Was this going to be a MOVIE NIGHT? Oh God, why did my hands have to be so clammy?

'*That's* what you watched together?' asked Jess sceptically the next day, as we sat in the dining room at lunch time. 'It sounds like the most snore film ever.'

'I think it sounds really good,' Danny said. Jess made a face at him.

'You would, Dweebface.'

'Don't call me Dweebface,' he groaned, looking round to check no one could hear. 'I am not a dweebface.'

'Why are you worried about someone overhearing me call you Dweebface?'

'Well, it's hardly attractive is it?'

'Who are you trying to attract?' Jess cackled, knocking his shoulder.

'Anna, back to the film,' he said, shoving Jess off him as she attempted to ruffle his curls.

'*Chariots of Fire*.' I nodded, swirling my glass of water distractedly.

Jess stared at me. 'Oh my God,' she cried, slamming down her own glass so that water spilt over the top on to her tray. 'Did you KISS last night?'

'*Jess*!' I pleaded, feeling the heat swamp my face. 'Do

you have to be so *loud*? No, we didn't kiss. Let's change the subject. Danny, do you have any scorpion facts for us today?'

'Well, actually, I did discover that –'

'Come on,' Jess wailed, interrupting Danny who grumpily returned to his food. 'A spontaneous movie night, he's trying to build your confidence, the lights are low . . .' Her eyes were practically bulging out of her head. 'You're not telling me he didn't even *try* to kiss you?'

'Uh,' I bit my lip. 'Well, I'm not sure.'

She looked confused. 'How can you not be sure? What happened?'

It had actually all started out very well. Dad was working, which meant that although normally he'd have been standing over us with his hawk-eye at all times, we were in the sitting room on our own.

Plus, when Connor had told Dad what film we were putting on, he'd approved completely. Granted, he'd also said, 'not very romantic, is it? That's all right by me!' just to make sure he embarrassed me as much as possible before he went back into his study. When I'd finished apologising for him, we sat down on the sofa, the bowl of popcorn consciously placed between us and Dog by my feet as usual.

Connor, as usual, was right: *Chariots of Fire* was

173

perfect. It actually made athletics seem interesting. I was completely hooked right from the beginning, and that's why I didn't really notice that Connor's hand had moved ever so slightly closer to mine until our fingers brushed.

'That was obviously when you started panicking,' Jess guessed correctly.

Yup. I'd panicked. Tingles were running up my arm and I didn't know what to do next. So I did my usual thing and just completely froze. 'There's a bit towards the end of the movie,' I told Jess and Danny. 'It's the best bit. One of the athletes, Eric Liddell, is running his race in the Olympics. There's a big build up and epic music and the camera pans around all the faces of his friends and teammates. You know when a film makes you just want to stand up and cheer?'

'Yup! Wow, I want to watch this film,' Danny nodded, stabbing at his macaroni. 'It sounds very intense.'

'Shut up, Danny!' Jess was gripping his arm. She nodded eagerly. 'Carry on.'

'Well, I cheered and then I turned to Connor and caught his eye, and he leaned towards me and . . .'

'AND?' Jess practically yelled.

And that's when the following happened:

1. Dog had woken up to the sounds of my cheering.

2. Dog got excited that I was cheering.

3. Dog thought I was cheering for him because of how awesome he is.

4. Dog jumped to his paws happily.

5. Dog leapt on top of me.

6. I got such a fright that I screamed and threw my arms out.

7. I hit Connor in the face. He cried out in pain.

8. Dad heard all the commotion and came running in from his study to see what was going on.

9. He saw Connor had been hit in the face. He saw me looking distraught. He saw Dog sitting on my lap on the sofa, in what he assumed was a protective position.

10. He bellowed, 'WHAT DID YOU TRY AND DO TO MY DAUGHTER, YOUNG MAN?'

Jess and Danny stared at me in silence. Danny had actually paused his fork halfway to his mouth. 'He said, "*what did you try and do to my daughter, young man?*"' Jess repeated, aghast.

'No, he *shouted* that. Obviously, once we'd explained everything he apologised.' I sighed. 'It's not too bad. I've spoken to Connor and he's fine with it. But yeah, the moment was ruined. There was absolutely no kissing, and I highly doubt that he's going to try again.'

'You need to stop hitting people in the face,' Danny advised.

'And screaming,' Jess added helpfully.

'I need to move to Antarctica where there are no people.'

'At least it was a good movie,' Danny offered.

'That's true,' I murmured, dejectedly following the rim of my glass with my finger.

'Did it make you more excited about being team captain?' Danny asked. 'Did it build your confidence?'

'Yeah, I guess it did.' I straightened up and took a deep breath. 'It got me thinking a lot about how we can get everyone else excited too. Maybe –'

'Hold it.' Jess was looking past my shoulder at someone who was coming our way. 'Looks like the Queen Bee's making a bee-line straight for us, Josie in tow as always. Get ready.'

I'd wondered how this week could possibly get any worse, and there it was. In a matter of seconds, Sophie and Josie were towering over me.

'Hello, Anna,' Sophie said curtly.

A hush descended upon the dining room, which wasn't surprising. The history between Sophie, Jess, Josie and I was well-known throughout the school.

'Hi, Sophie, how are you?' I squeaked. I prayed that

she had just come over to ask for the salt.

'I wanted to let you know that Josie and I know what you've been up to. It's outrageous.'

'What?' I blinked up at them.

Then I froze. Could Connor have told them? Had Sophie come over to tell me off for slapping him in the face? In front of the WHOLE SCHOOL?

I really would have to move to Antarctica, I decided. There was just no other option. I hoped Helena would lend me one of her big fluffy coats. I know how cold it gets there.

'The other day,' Sophie angled her body so that she was addressing her whole audience rather than just me, 'I went to the Sports department, and do you know what Miss Clifford told me? That you,' she pointed her long perfectly manicured finger in my face, 'had taken a box of athletics equipment. That you had, in fact, been taking it pretty much every other lunch time since we came back from half term. You've obviously been tampering with it! And I'm going to go and see Miss Duke about it immediately!'

Jess suddenly exploded with laughter. 'Sophie, you crack me up!'

'I don't see what's so funny, Jessica. This is very serious! The team captain of the Puffins has been using dirty methods to try to secure a win for her loser team!'

'Oh really?' Jess cackled. 'Tell us, Sophie, how would she know which equipment would be used by the Eagles and which by the Puffins? I'm pretty sure we all use the same stuff.'

'Well, maybe . . .' Sophie searched for an answer to Jess's valid point. 'Maybe all the Puffins know something that we don't! Maybe you're going to instruct them about it!'

'Yeah,' Josie jumped in, trying to be helpful to her leader, 'because loser teams have to stick together.'

'THAT'S IT.' Maybe I was feeling particularly inspired by *Chariots of Fire*, or maybe I'd had enough of being told that I was a loser not just by the press but now by Sophie and Josie, but suddenly something snapped. I jumped to my feet, my chair skidding backwards. Even Jess stopped laughing and stared.

'Will you both STOP calling my team the "loser team"?' I demanded, pointing my non-manicured, chipped-thanks-to-all-the-discus-throwing nail right back in Sophie's face. 'Yes, I've been taking a box of equipment at lunchtimes, because I've been training with James Tyndale for all my events.' Sophie and Josie whipped their heads round to look at James, as did everyone else in the room. He became very focused on moving his food round his plate.

'You've been . . . *training*?' Sophie sneered. Josie began sniggering behind her.

'Yes, Sophie, I've been training, and let me tell you something: I'm getting good. Or at least less terrible. So you Eagles better watch your backs, because this year things are going to change.' I could feel myself really warming up. I stood up on my chair to address the whole room. In my head I was totally Eric Liddell making a rousing speech to the British Olympics squad. 'This year the underdog is up to the challenge. This year we are stronger than we have ever been. This year the Puffins are going to win!'

The room erupted into cheers and applause, and I grinned. James saluted me from next to a very disgruntled-looking Brendan, and out of the corner of my eye I saw Connor staring up at me. I hoped he was impressed.

I was actually kind of impressed at myself. Maybe I should have considered making 'being good at speeches' my thing. Anna The Orator totally had a ring to it.

But then I remembered the time that Mum had told me to get up and say something at one of Dad's birthday dinner parties and I'd stood up, taken a deep breath and inhaled the gum that I'd forgotten I was chewing. I'd started choking and almost died.

'I'm not threatened by you, Anna Huntley,' Sophie

announced loudly as I climbed down from my chair. 'You have the sporting prowess of a snail. No amount of training can change that.'

'I may not have natural physical ability, Sophie,' I said, lifting my tray from the table, 'but I have the mindset of Eric Liddell.'

'Eric who?'

'Duh, Eric Liddell,' I repeated, putting my tray in the rack and strolling towards the exit where Connor still stood, watching intently. As I walked out with my head held high, I finished the conversation without even looking back. 'It's from *Chariots of Fire*. You might want to look it up.'

And OK, maybe I tripped up as I left the room, but I didn't even care. I felt amazing.

From: anna_huntley@zingmail.co.uk
To: [Puffins]
Subject: PUFFIN PARTY!

Dear fellow Puffin,

It is my pleasure to invite you to:

THE PUFFIN PARTY!

On the evening exams finish, please join your team captain at her house for Puffin-themed fun and games. Details to follow, but please save the date.

THE PUFFINS SHALL PREVAIL!
RSVP: anna_huntley@zingmail.co.uk

From: jess.delby@zingmail.co.uk
To: anna_huntley@zingmail.co.uk
Subject: The Puffin party

Dude. That is the BEST idea.

J x

From: anna_huntley@zingmail.co.uk
To: jess.delby@zingmail.co.uk
Subject: Re: The Puffin party

I can't take the credit for this one, it was James's idea.
He said that my earlier run-in with Sophie inspired him to
think about how we can raise the morale of the Puffins. He
thought a Puffin Party might be a good team-spirit-building
thing.

Love, me xxx

From: jess.delby@zingmail.co.uk
To: anna_huntley@zingmail.co.uk

Subject: Re: The Puffin party

Well, here is my RSVP:

COUNT ME IN, CAPTAIN!

J x

PS I think you should go as a puffin. Just a thought.

From: Tyndale@bouncemail.co.uk
To: anna_huntley@zingmail.co.uk
Subject: Great invitation

Nicely done, we've never had an actual team party before, just boring things like a bake sale. Was your dad OK in the end about holding it at your house?

I think you're doing a great job of building your confidence. You're great. We'll win.

James.

From: anna_huntley@zingmail.co.uk
To: Tyndale@bouncemail.co.uk

Subject: Re: Great invitation

Thank you, James, that is very kind. I am extremely talented when it comes to athletics. Some people have it, some people don't.

Eric Liddell and I have it.

I wish he was still alive so we could come together and discuss the drawbacks of being so remarkable.

Anna.

From: Tyndale@bouncemail.co.uk
To: anna_huntley@zingmail.co.uk
Subject: Re: Great invitation

Were you just making fun of my heartfelt encouragement?

James.

From: anna_huntley@zingmail.co.uk
To: jess.delby@zingmail.co.uk
Subject: HELP

I just made fun of James Tyndale over email, totally forgetting that he is one of the most popular guys in the year and we're not really friends.

I actually FORGOT.

What do I do?

Love, me xxx

From: jess.delby@zingmail.co.uk
To: anna_huntley@zingmail.co.uk
Subject: Re: HELP

What did he say?

J x

From: anna_huntley@zingmail.co.uk
To: jess.delby@zingmail.co.uk
Subject: Re: HELP

He said, 'are you making fun of my heartfelt encouragement?'

Love, me xxx

From: jess.delby@zingmail.co.uk
To: anna_huntley@zingmail.co.uk
Subject: Re: HELP

Reply saying, 'Yes, moron.'

From: anna_huntley@zingmail.co.uk
To: Tyndale@bouncemail.co.uk
Subject: Re: Great invitation

Yes, moron.

From: jess.delby@zingmail.co.uk
To: anna_huntley@zingmail.co.uk
Subject: Re: HELP

Haha, only joking. Imagine if you did send that! Remember
that he is your coach, and if you want us to win this thing,
you need to keep him on-side. Maybe say something cool,
like, 'No, just messing around before I do some pre-training
sit-ups!'

You're welcome.

J x

From: anna_huntley@zingmail.co.uk
To: jess.delby@zingmail.co.uk
Subject: Re: HELP

I HATE YOU.

Love, me xxx

From: connorlawrence1@zingmail.co.uk
To: anna_huntley@zingmail.co.uk
Subject: Puffin Invitation

Hey Spidey,

Just dropping you a line to say that I was so impressed
with the way you stood up to Sophie at lunch today. I think
the Puffin party sounds brilliant. I'll definitely try to be
there.

Glad to see you channelling your inner Eric Liddell too.
Thanks for having me over for the film, I had a really good
time. I hope you did too?

Connor

From: anna_huntley@zingmail.co.uk
To: jess.delby@zingmail.co.uk
Subject: Re: HELP

Oh God. Now Connor is emailing me!!!! He's asking if I had a good time when we watched *Chariots of Fire*. What do I reply???

Love, me xxx

From: jess.delby@zingmail.co.uk
To: anna_huntley@zingmail.co.uk
Subject: Re: HELP

You know, last time I helped you, I got a VERY rude reply with no explanation and now you're asking for my help again! Talk about hot and cold.

Say something funny, like, 'No?' He'll find that hilarious.

J x

From: anna_huntley@zingmail.co.uk
To: connorlawrence1@zingmail.co.uk

Subject: Re: Puffin Invitation

No?

Anna

From: jess.delby@zingmail.co.uk
To: anna_huntley@zingmail.co.uk
Subject: Re: HELP

HA. I'm hilarious. Obviously I'm joking again. Hmm, let's take time with this reply. You want to let him know that you had a good time, but you don't want to sound overly keen (even though you are). You don't want to jump straight in there, especially after you slapped him in the face when he tried to kiss you.

Maybe say something along the lines of, 'Yeah, it was fun, we should do it again sometime.'

You know, nice and chilled.

J x

From: anna_huntley@zingmail.co.uk

To: jess.delby@zingmail.co.uk
Subject: Re: HELP

I sent the emails. The emails you were joking about. Both of them. Before I got your emails saying they were jokes.

From: jess.delby@zingmail.co.uk
To: anna_huntley@zingmail.co.uk
Subject: Re: HELP

Oh. Yeah, that's really bad.

What are you going to do?

J x

From: anna_huntley@zingmail.co.uk
To: jess.delby@zingmail.co.uk
Subject: Re: HELP

Do you think if I moved to Antarctica the penguins would accept me as one of their own?

From: jess.delby@zingmail.co.uk
To: anna_huntley@zingmail.co.uk

Subject: Re: HELP

Probably not.

J x

From: anna_huntley@zingmail.co.uk
To: jess.delby@zingmail.co.uk
Subject: Re: HELP

It's got to be better than being at school though, right?

From: jess.delby@zingmail.co.uk
To: anna_huntley@zingmail.co.uk
Subject: Re: HELP

Definitely.

J x

How the people in my life react to stress, created for potential use in social studies of the future:

Dad
It's all about the eyebrows for Dad. Once they've taken on a life of their own there's no stopping them, no matter how many times you tell him that everything will be fine and his bride-to-be will come to her senses.

Lesson learnt: Reminding Dad that he was the one who caused this stress in the first place — no one asked him to propose — does not help. It only leads to further eyebrow jolting and a strongly-worded request to leave his study. Geez.

Mum
Lots of shouting and drama. For example the time her computer broke and she was on a deadline for

a newspaper. She was so dismayed that she yelled at the computer screen for ages and then, when that didn't help, tore the keyboard from its cord and threw it in her bin.

Lesson learnt: Don't pretend to know how to put a keyboard cord back into its keyboard. It's better to admit straight away that you have no idea what to do, otherwise you'll be fiddling away clumsily for an hour while Mum taps her foot impatiently and rants about how technology is warping our minds.

Danny
Oh my goodness, the curls. I thought I had seen them at their most wild, but clearly I knew nothing. Exam week set Danny's nerves at breaking point and his hair became an indestructible blond-ringlet perm from the 80s.

Lesson learnt: Do not ping the curls. Much like the Hulk, Danny suddenly forgets whether you're friend or foe when you ping a curl. It also does not help at all if you cry 'BOING!' really loudly when you ping it.

Jess

When her Art project was due, Jess behaved as though the thoughts in her head were moving round too quickly to translate properly into speech. She adopted mannerisms similar to those of a nutty professor, waving her hands around wildly, clicking her pens irritably and muttering things that only she could understand.

Lesson learnt: Don't try to lighten the tension by jumping out at her from behind a pillar. Jess screamed her head off and then hit me over the head with her Art folder several times.

Marianne

It turns out that Marianne, who is usually as cool as a cucumber, can find certain things extremely stressful, for example her mother booking a circus act for her wedding. Under extreme pressure Marianne becomes cold and introverted, and asking her a simple question such as, 'do you like my jazzy new sweatband, M-dawg?' led to a vicious you-are-too-much-of-a-freak-for-me-to-handle-right-now stare.

Lesson learnt: Don't try out your limited repertoire of jokes on her. It will make her hate you more.

Dog
When stressed, Dog brings you things that you're not sure you own. He also climbs into the dryer and barks manically at inanimate objects such as plugs.

Lesson learnt: Best not to try to calm Dog by playing that weird whale-sound CD Mum bought me. Instead of calming him, it makes him lie on his back and pant heavily in terror.

Myself
It is difficult to judge, of course, but if pressed I would claim that I am remarkably calm and collected, even under huge amounts of pressure — much more so, I might say, then my fellow students. On top of normal teenage worries such as end-of-term exams, I have the added pressure of convincing everyone that I am a born-again Eric Liddell who will lead her team to victory.

Also, I accidentally insult every boy who tries to talk to me, including the boy I like and I have the press watching my every move in case I fall into a plant pot again. In spite all of this, I am extremely affable, unruffled and an utter pleasure to be around.

'I CAN'T HANDLE THE PRESSURE!' I yelled, slinging my school bag across the floor. As if in slow-mo I watched as it crashed into a table, knocking over the vase on top which smashed into smithereens all over the floor.

Fenella stared at the broken pieces of the vase as the water from the flowers trickled across Helena's marble hall. Then she sniffed and wrote something down on her clipboard. She turned on her heel and walked into the sitting room, and two members of her wedding team came into the hall carrying a broom and mop.

'Whoops,' I laughed nervously as they began sweeping up the pieces. 'I can do that.'

'We deal with this kind of thing all the time,' one of them told me. 'You go on in.'

Apologising profusely, I edged into the sitting room. Fenella stood in the corner, barking orders into her headset, and Marianne sat on the sofa playing on her phone. There were two more members of the wedding team sitting next to her, laptops on their laps, glancing up apprehensively at Fenella as if waiting for their next instruction.

'What was that crash?' Marianne asked, spotting me.

'I knocked over a vase.'

'Did you fall into it?'

'No,' I said bitterly.

'That makes a change.'

'Look, it got in the way of my bag.'

Marianne snorted, barely looking up from her phone. 'What's happening now? More Connor drama?'

'More drama full stop!' I collapsed on to the sofa next to her. 'End of term exams aside, everyone at school now knows I've been training with James Tyndale. There's even MORE pressure for me not to kill anyone with a discus on sports day.'

'I see.'

'On top of all that I accidentally hit Connor in the face the other day when we were watching a movie together, and I insulted both him and James over email. Dad is running around the house yelling all the time, his study is practically drowning in paper, and Dog keeps trying to make everyone happy by bringing us totally inappropriate gifts.'

'Like?' Marianne prompted, looking very amused.

'He brought me someone's pet ferret yesterday.'

Her eyes widened and she opened her mouth. Then we heard footsteps upstairs. 'Mum's up there with your mum and the dresser.' Marianne shut her eyes. 'I can't believe we have to do this now.'

'You don't think it'll be fun?'

'Are you kidding?'

'We're trying on bridesmaid dresses. I've seen it in the movies. It's a perfect time for female bonding, and that's what we all need right now.'

'No, we need space from the wedding madness right now.'

I narrowed my eyes at her. 'Positive vibes, Marianne. Were you not just listening to my tales of woe? I would appreciate it if you could not add to the stress in my life and instead embrace this lovely evening of fun. We might actually get excited about the wedding once we're dressed up nicely.' I sighed. 'Plus it will be nice to hang out with you and Helena. I hardly get to see her these days.'

'She's never been like this before, you know. Seriously. I think, and bear with me here,' she took a deep breath, 'I think she really cares about this one. It's like, this is THE one, THE wedding.'

'Well, that's how it should be! Celebrities . . .'

'You know what I mean,' Marianne scowled. 'The other ones were stupid, but this one she's taking seriously.

197

She wants it to be perfect because it's Nick.'

'She should tell him that,' I said. 'He's been getting very upset by it all. He thinks she's getting a bit carried away. If he knew it was because she cares so much then it might help. I think he thinks it's just because she's . . . you know . . . famous.'

'I told her that she's pushing him away and that she should make time for a date night or something, but it's like her mind has been taken over by a wedding demon.' Marianne glanced at the wedding team. They were pretending not to listen.

There was a commotion in the hall, and we heard Helena and my mum coming downstairs, talking at about a hundred miles an hour and sounding as though they weren't listening to a word the other one was saying. They bustled into the room and Helena clapped her hands in excitement. 'Do we have a treat in store for you!' she sang, beaming, as the dresser followed her.

Then one of the wedding team wheeled in a coat rack packed with suspiciously pouffy bags. They had to be full of bridesmaid dresses. I got a sinking feeling about what lay ahead, but I tried to disguise it.

'Exciting!' I enthused.

Marianne gripped my hand. Worryingly, Mum wouldn't look me in the eye.

The dresser pulled down the zip of the first bag, and for a few seconds I couldn't work out if I was looking at a dress or a life-sized yellow pompom.

'Isn't it splendid?' Helena squealed. Apparently she had lost the ability to see. 'Come on, Anna, try it on.'

I didn't even have the chance to protest. The wedding team helped me up – I mean they physically lifted me out of my seat and pulled me behind a screen specifically set up for the occasion. 'I don't think this is for me!' I yelped as they started yanking the monstrosity over my head. I was finally squeezed into the mountains of stiff netting, my arms sticking out at odd angles.

I shrieked, but they had already pulled the screen away so that everyone could see the result. I caught sight of myself in the mirror. 'I LOOK LIKE BIG BIRD.'

'I don't think it's on right,' Helena said thoughtfully. Marianne burst into howls of laughter and even Mum got the giggles. 'Are you sure her head is through the right hole?'

'MARIANNE'S TURN!' I cried, flailing my arms around in a desperate attempt to get out of the thing.

'Hmm, I don't think that one quite suits the theme I'm going for,' Helena remarked.

'Not unless the theme is SESAME STREET!' I yelled. 'A little help, please?' I tried to turn round to get back behind the screen but instead just fell over, face down on to the floor.

Luckily it didn't hurt – the mounds of netting cushioned my fall. I practically bounced upright again.

When I finally got out of the dress, I was so traumatised that I curled up next to Mum and clung on to her for dear life. But I soon felt better – Marianne appeared from behind the screen in what could only be described as a curtain.

'I think it's sweet!' Helena protested as I shrieked with laughter. 'It comes with a matching bonnet!'

Marianne gasped in horror as Helena held out the offending hat. 'Not a chance!' she cried, and fled back behind the screen. She reappeared with a face of thunder and sat down on the sofa in a massive strop.

'I think you looked marvellous,' I sniggered, and then wilted under the icy glare I received in return.

'Don't worry, darlings,' Helena smiled brightly, selecting another bag from the rail. 'We've got three more racks to go!'

Marianne leaned forward and started banging her head on the coffee table.

19

Reasons why I will never listen to Jess Delby's advice again:

1. She once said that I looked good in a sparkly headband. Then I got home, after wearing it at school ALL DAY, and my dad said in this really rude voice, 'were you auditioning for a disco music video today, then?' You know something is really wrong when your own father mocks you.

2. She once persuaded me to try the monkey bars, even though I categorically told her I couldn't do them. I don't care what the doctor said, my wrist was DEFINITELY broken.

3. She once insisted that my dad would find a prank call hilarious because he has a 'great sense of humour'. I was grounded for three days after Dad was gullible enough to believe (a) that the Prime Minister's secretary had the voice of a fourteen-year-old and (b) that the Prime Minister would actually be interested in anything Dad had to say.

4. She once assured me that it was fine to put foil

in the microwave. Thankfully we were at her house, otherwise I might really have a reputation for fire-starting.

And the most important reason why I will never listen to her advice again:

5. She persuaded me to dress up as a puffin for the Puffin Party.

In her defence, I had so many opportunities to turn round and say to her, 'Jess? I think it is a simply hilarious idea to dress up in a puffin suit for a Puffin Party, but you know what? Connor is probably going to be there, as he's a Puffin and everything, so I think I'm going to give it a miss and dress up in a super nice outfit instead, so he'll fall madly in love with me again.'

Instead, like a DOOFUS, I trailed along with her to the costume-hire shop where they had a full-on puffin suit with webbed plastic orange feet, its big head thing complete with a beak and everything. And she was so excited when I tried it on that I just went along with it, laughing all the way home. I imagined how wonderful everyone would think I was, and how they would all think I was so dedicated to the Puffin team.

That's how Jess persuaded me. 'They'll all think you're hilarious, Anna,' she said. 'You'll look so confident and cool. Boys love a girl with a sense of humour, they don't want someone who only cares about their appearance. Trust me, all the boys on our team will fall head over heels for you.'

Yes, Jess, you're right. All the boys will fall head over heels. LITERALLY. BECAUSE THEY WILL BE LAUGHING SO HARD AT ME THEY WILL LOSE THEIR BALANCE.

At least it made Dad brighten up for a bit. When I came plodding down the stairs, careful not to knock anything over with my big wings and peering out from underneath the large hooked beak curling over my head, Dad took one look at me and the stress of his life just lifted completely.

He hadn't been over the moon about the party before – but he hadn't really had a choice in the matter. I had mentioned it to him on one of the rare occasions that Helena had been round. 'Don't be such a bore, Nicholas,' she had lectured when I announced my party plans. 'I think it's a great idea – it's so wonderful to see Anna take on such an important challenge. She should have her parents' full support.'

He couldn't say anything after that, could he?

But then my puffin costume just about made his whole year. 'You look . . . you look,' he said, as he gasped for breath, 'let me go and get my camera, don't you move, don't you move!'

I should have known then. I should have thought to myself, *if my dad finds it this funny, then I should probably take the puffin suit off.* But I was so excited to see him happy that I didn't think of my dignity. Instead I lumbered around, barely able to see but thrilled that I had managed to cheer up my miserable father.

My mum's reaction should have been another giveaway. Arriving laden with bird-themed cups, plates and decorations, she took one look at me and put her hand on her heart as though it was a big moment in our mother-daughter relationship. 'Darling,' she announced, 'you look splendid. Simply mesmerising!'

This from a woman who once came down dressed for a party, and I saw her and said, 'Wow, Mum! You look amazing! You've really gone all out on the pirate theme.' Then it turned out that there was absolutely no theme at all.

Dog's reaction should finally have made me see my error. He was being looked after by one of our neighbours for the evening – I didn't want him to get hurt by someone dancing violently, and Dad unfairly didn't trust him not to eat everything. He was being led out of the house when I came to say goodbye to him for the evening. He took one look at me in the puffin costume and pelted away down the road at full speed.

When Jess finally turned up I dragged her straight up to my room (which in massive puffin feet is no easy task, let me tell you). I tripped up the stairs at least three times and almost permanently squashed the beak.

'HOW did I let you persuade me to do this?' I asked. 'I look stupid!'

'No, you look amazing!' she cried, sitting down on my bed and re-doing her lip gloss.

Jess had, of course, come dressed the way everyone else would. She looked gorgeous in a black skirt and pretty, figure-hugging red top. She had done these really cute stripes on her cheeks too, in orange, white and black, the Puffin colours. I couldn't even be angry at her.

'Anna, honestly? I think you're the coolest person ever for wearing the puffin suit. This raises you to, like, legendary status.'

I hesitated. 'Really? Legendary?'

'Legendary,' she nodded sincerely, a firm hand on my wing.

And I fell for it AGAIN! Jess should really consider taking over the world – she is very clever and cunning, and people just do what she says.

The party started, and I began to greet people at the door. It wasn't too bad at first – although I was getting some odd stares from people – but then Stephanie showed up at my door. She was with Danny, the traitor, and her blunt-cut fringe looked incredible. 'Oh.' I stared at her. 'Hello, Stephanie.'

Danny raised a critical eyebrow at my tone but Stephanie didn't seem to have noticed anything weird.

'I know I'm not a Puffin, but Danny and Connor said I might be able to come along,' she explained cheerfully. 'I hope you don't mind. I feel like an honorary member of your team, I wish I could swap! You look great, by the way.'

I craned round her, looking for Connor. My heart sank when I couldn't see him.

'Right.'

'You must be wondering where Connor is – he got a little held up but he's going to try to come later.'

I wanted to give her a fake-sympathetic look and say sweetly, 'Oh, Stephanie, I'm so sorry – but it really is Puffins only. Bye-bye!' But 1) I'm not that brave and 2) I didn't want her to tell Connor that I had been mean to her.

So I settled for sending Puffin death stares at her

back as she and Danny made their way into the party, chatting happily.

'You look like you're about to lay an egg, Huntley.' James appeared by my side, handing me a cup of the fruit punch that my mum had made especially for the party.

'Oh, well, yeah. I'm just feeling a bit grumpy that my wings keep getting in the way,' I bluffed, not very convincingly.

James laughed. 'Well, it's still an awesome costume. I wish you'd told me. I would have dressed to match.'

'Har har.' I rolled my eyes, but of course because of the stupid costume he couldn't see. I pushed the beak up a bit so that he could peer in.

'You've done a good job at ruffling the Eagles' feathers. Pun intended,' he smirked. 'And everyone here is way more enthusiastic about sports day than they were last year. Thanks to you, they really think we can win!'

'No pressure, then,' I gulped, watching as Jess enthusiastically did the Octopus on the dance floor.

'Jess looks like she's having fun,' James commented.

'I taught her that move,' I told him. James raised his eyebrows. I think he was impressed. 'But in this costume it's a bit hard to achieve.'

'Really?' he asked as more people joined her on the dance floor.

'Oh, yeah. There's no room to manoeuvre,' I said, stiffly raising a wing to show what I meant. 'And I don't want to injure anyone.'

Jess saw us and started pulling an imaginary rope to get me over to her. For someone so cool, she has some very cheesy dance moves.

'Come on, how can you resist her?' James asked, grabbing a wing and pulling me over to the dance floor.

It turned out that I could dance, sort of, although I almost took out Jess and James before they realised that I needed more room to move about. Suddenly, despite the puffin suit, I was enjoying myself. I even forgave Danny a little bit for letting Stephanie tag along. I saw them laughing together in a corner of the lounge. She didn't seem too lost without Connor.

'I'm going to go get my camera!' Jess suddenly announced above the music. 'Keep on throwing those puffin moves!'

James and I continued jumping about. He made me laugh by flicking my beak and I got him back by shimmying my bottom at him. On a roll, I spun round for one last wriggle – and stopped in my tracks.

Connor was standing in the doorway of the sitting room, and he was looking pretty hurt. I looked at James and then around at the otherwise empty dance floor (my puffin moves had been pretty wild) and realised what it must look like.

'Hey, Con –' I began, and then my stomach dropped as Connor just turned away to where Stephanie was sitting. She leapt up to hug him.

'You OK, Anna?' James asked. He had stopped dancing too.

'Yeah,' I nodded, still looking at Connor with Stephanie. 'I just need to tell . . . well, I just need to go say hi to . . . um, someone.'

'Anna,' James grabbed hold of my wing. 'I think you should say something.'

'I think so too.'

'Wait, I'll get everyone's attention.'

'Huh?' Was he MAD? I couldn't tell Connor how I felt when EVERYONE was listening! This wasn't an American romcom!

But before I could tell James that, he had already switched the music off. I stood there, completely mute, as everyone looked around, wondering why it had gone quiet.

'Everyone!' James said to the room. I was completely frozen. How could I make a quick getaway? The puffin costume was too conspicuous! WHY WAS I WEARING THIS THING AGAIN?

'Our captain would like to make a speech about sports day!'

Oh.

I quickly put on a smile – not that anyone could see it under the beak – and waited for the cheers to die down.

'Hello, everyone.' I racked my brain for something inspirational. I looked round at James to tell me what to say, but he just gestured for me to carry on. 'Uh . . . right. I've actually been doing some research on puffins. The thing about puffins is, they're actually a very impressive bird. For example, they can carry loads of fish in their beaks, they can dive under water *and* they can beat their wings so fast that they become a blur.'

People looked a little bit confused but then I saw Jess mouthing, 'GEEK!' before grinning and giving me a thumbs-up. I carried on.

'And that, my Puffin friends, is how the Eagles are going to see us on sports day: as a blur as we race past them towards the winning trophy!'

Everyone burst into applause, cheering and stomping, but as I stood in the middle of it all, I realised the person that mattered most of all, Connor, was the one voice I couldn't hear. I peered through the orange, white and black-striped faces of the party to see Connor waving goodbye to Stephanie and Danny and just walking out of the door.

I guess I should be grateful that when I was pulling my pants out of the Hoover bag on my doorstep, it was James who came round the corner and saw me, not Connor.

Not that I was particularly happy about ANYONE seeing me in that situation – but after what happened at the party, I didn't think Connor could cope with any more weirdness from me.

I'd checked my phone almost every ten seconds since the moment I woke up the next morning, but I'd had nothing from him. He had clearly got the wrong impression at the party when he saw me dancing with James on our own. But we hadn't been slow dancing or anything, and the fact that I had been in a puffin costume at the time had made the moment super unromantic. I just had to tell Connor that. I had decided that after I'd found my pants I'd go over to his house and explain everything.

Of course, I didn't realise that James would make an appearance that morning. I thought I might get a day off from my sports day training considering I'd thrown such a motivational party the night before. That was why I took the risk of going outside to fish my pants out of the Hoover bag. I had obviously checked for photographers first and, seeing the coast was clear, tottered right on out in my SNOOPY DRESSING GOWN, without any idea that James was jogging round the corner at that moment.

It was all Dad's fault.

He had been totally unfair, ordering me to tidy my bedroom as soon as I came downstairs that morning. He was having a big fight with Helena in our kitchen and they wanted me out the way. 'But, Dad!' I protested. 'I'm meant to be bathing in my glory as team captain of the Puffins!'

'You can bathe in your glory once you've tidied your room and you've actually won something,' he growled, Helena tapping her nails impatiently on the kitchen counter. I knew I should leave them to it, but it was my house too. Anyway, they didn't seem to do anything but argue these days. Quite frankly, I felt that I was being generous not calling child services to tell them about the wedding torture I was being subjected to.

'I don't know anyone else whose parents would make them clean their room the morning after they threw a big party,' I huffed, whipping up the hood of my Snoopy dressing gown so its ears flopped forward.

'I don't know anyone else whose children would get to

go to the new *Avengers* film premiere on a school night.'

'OK, firstly that was yonks ago, and secondly you can't keep pulling that out of the bag whenever you want me to do something.'

'Go tidy your room, Anna, it's disgraceful. It will take you one hour maximum. GO.'

'FINE!' I grumped, and attempted to stalk out of the room.

I say *attempted* because as I swished my dressing gown like a cloak behind me, Dog went for it. He tugged on the bottom and yanked me backwards. I ended up having to drag him along with me, my dressing gown clutched in his jaws.

'Do you see what you are doing to him?!' I cried as Dad and Helena watched in silence. Then Dog suddenly released my dressing gown and I lurched forward out of the room.

When we were out of their sight, I was so angry that I gave Dog Dad's BlackBerry to play with.

This is where karma bit me on the bottom. I took the Hoover upstairs and I danced around my room with it, singing along to some old Queen songs. And mid-way through 'Bohemian Rhapsody', I accidentally Hoovered up a pair of my pants.

I could have just let them go – but they happened to

be one of my favourite pairs, the ones with Odie from *Garfield* on them. I yelled at Dad, but he was completely unsympathetic to my plight. 'For goodness' sake, Anna,' he cried, leaning on my door frame, having thundered up the stairs when I refused to stop yelling. 'You made all this racket because you Hoovered up a pair of Odie pants? I thought you'd hurt yourself or something!'

'What do I do?' I wailed. 'You have to get them out for me.'

'I do not. You can get them out yourself. Just take the Hoover bag outside and fish them out.'

'OUTSIDE?! In my DRESSING GOWN?!'

'Yes, outside, Anna,' he grumbled, heading back down the stairs to restart his argument. 'I don't want the dust in the house.'

I grumbled about how unfair he was being as I got out the stupid bag from the stupid Hoover and took it out the stupid house, holding it away from Dog's reach.

That was precisely the moment when James came round the corner.

'What are you doing, exactly?' he asked.

'Nothing,' I huffed, quickly shoving the pants back into the Hoover bag, which released a massive puff of dust in my face. I coughed and spluttered and James waved it away.

'Did you Hoover something up?'

214

'No, of course not. Don't be stupid.'

'Looks like that's exactly what you did. Come on, what was it?'

'No! I'm just, you know . . .' I tried to think quickly.

'Rummaging about in the Hoover bag for no reason?'

'How come you're here?' I asked, trying to look casual, like I held Hoover bags on my front doorstep all the time.

'What does it look like?' He gestured at his running gear. 'Come on, out of that . . . uh . . . dressing gown and on with your trainers.'

'No way! It's my day off.'

'Winners don't get a day off.'

'Oh please, did you get that from a motivational lecture or something?'

'Come on,' he grinned. 'I know you want to.'

'I really don't.'

Just at that moment, the now familiar sound of Dad and Helena arguing drifted out of the house. 'Actually,' I said, 'now you mention it, maybe I could force myself to go on one quick run. For the sake of *the team*. Give me five minutes.'

'Sounds like everyone is having fun in your house today,' James commented when I'd made it back out again at warp speed.

'You don't know the half of it . . .' I started. And then all of a sudden, even though I hadn't been planning on offloading all the woes of my life on to James, they just came tumbling out.

'And now,' I concluded, throwing my arms up in distress, 'I don't even know if my dad *wants* a wedding. I mean, he still loves her and all that stuff but I'm worried that the circus suggestion was the last straw. And I really like Helena and Marianne – they're family now.'

James looked thoughtful. 'Well, no wonder you've got your trainers on the wrong feet, Anna. You've got a lot going on.'

I stopped and looked down at my feet. 'Dang it! You could have told me!'

I ignored his smirk as I bent down to switch shoes. 'James, can I tell you a secret?'

'Another one? What am I, your therapist?'

'I'm a little bit terrified about sports day.'

'That's not a secret, Anna. Whenever I mention it your face goes really weird. I can literally hear your stomach churning.'

'There's just so much pressure! Everyone needs me to do well, but I'm just so bad!'

'No you're not! You've really improved,' he insisted, putting a hand on my shoulder and giving it a shake.

'Seriously, Anna, you're good enough. You don't need to win everything. It's a points-based system, remember? The most important thing is that you've given everyone else motivation. The Puffins really, really want to win now. Usually we just resign ourselves to losing.'

'You think so?'

'We have a good shot this year. I know it.'

'Right! I need to stay focused, just like Eric.'

'Exactly! Feel the spirit of your Eric Liddell person and you'll have wings on your shoes.'

'You really must tell me which motivational lecture you attended. It sounds like there were some corkers.'

'Oh, shut up and get running.'

By the time we did a final sprint home I didn't even care whether Dad and Helena were still arguing. I was too exhausted. I rang the doorbell, panting.

'It'll be worth it when you have that trophy,' James puffed, bending over and putting his hands on his knees. 'Keep your eyes on the prize, It Girl.'

Dad answered the door. He saw me standing there and said, without checking to see if I was alone, 'Anna! You've been a long while fishing your *Garfield* pants out of the Hoover bag.'

James slowly pulled himself up and looked at me wide-eyed, before he burst into side-splitting laughter.

From: jess.delby@zingmail.co.uk
To: anna_huntley@zingmail.co.uk
Subject: Seriously

Why do you even OWN Odie pants?

J x

From: anna_huntley@zingmail.co.uk
To: jess.delby@zingmail.co.uk
Subject: Re: Seriously

Do you think my authority as team captain is still intact?

Love, me xxx

From: jess.delby@zingmail.co.uk
To: anna_huntley@zingmail.co.uk
Subject: Re: Seriously

No.

J x

On the day before sports day, the Connor situation got even worse.

School was buzzing about the Puffin-Eagle rivalry. No one could concentrate on anything else. Even the teachers were getting excited, asking us in lessons who was going to win. Just walking down the corridor was like walking through *High School Musical*, and I don't want to make any accusations but I'm pretty sure that when I passed the staff room I saw something on the whiteboard that looked *very* much like some kind of betting system.

Even lunch became a battle of loyalties. People like James struggled to work out where they should sit. He stopped at our table on the way to Brendan's to relate his internal struggle. 'It feels wrong to sit with the Eagles.'

'James,' I put down my fork, 'they're your *friends*. Granted, they're not people I would choose to sit with – especially Josie or Sophie . . .' I lost my train of thought. 'But anyway . . . oh yes, they're not actually your enemies. It's just sports day.'

Jess kicked me hard in the shin. 'OW!' I cried.

'They ARE our enemies until after sports day,' Jess corrected, looking extremely smug with herself while I rubbed my leg and stared at her angrily. 'If you sit with them, James, try and discover their tactics.'

'He's not a spy, Jessica.'

'He is now.' She narrowed her eyes at James. 'Remember whose side you're on.'

James nodded gravely and went to sit down as Danny shook his head at Jess, chortling. 'What are you laughing at, Mr I-Don't-Believe-in-Competitive-Sport?' Jess asked, glaring at him.

'This is all just so ridiculous. I actually think it's kind of fun.' Danny pointed his fork at me. 'This is all your fault, Anna. You're the one who started it. Now the whole school is gearing up for a big showdown.' He smiled. 'I can't wait for tomorrow.'

I tried to swallow the lump that had suddenly formed in my throat, and glanced around the room to see if Connor was there. I still hadn't had the chance to talk to him about the party. Danny was right, the whole school was geared up for tomorrow. I knew I had to be, too, but it was hard to get enthusiastic when I had mucked things up so badly with Connor. He was the main reason I'd gone for captain in the first place. I'd been trying to prove to him that he shouldn't give up on me – but maybe he had already.

I glanced towards Brendan's table as James slid his tray down next to him. As he did so, Sophie flicked her hair back and stared pointedly over her shoulder at me. It was amazing how inferior she could make me feel with just a look.

'You're going down, Sophie,' Jess hissed, watching her.

'She can't hear you, Jess,' Danny said. 'Unless you shout it across the room and really scare her.'

'Don't you DARE!' I stood up. 'I need to go for some air. I feel nervous.'

'Do what you have to do, Captain. We're all behind you.' Jess nodded solemnly.

I rolled my eyes at Danny then headed towards the exit as quickly as possible. But not quickly enough.

A group of Puffins from the year below spotted me approaching and burst into a chant of, 'PU-FFINS! PU-FFINS!'

Others soon joined in and then, of course, the Eagles had to respond. 'EA-GLES! EA-GLES!'

People started banging on the tables as well, and the noise became overwhelming. I sprinted out of the dining room – these days my speed was actually respectable. I burst through the main doors and into the sunshine, running round the school building until I got to an empty bench. Or so I thought.

'Anna?'

I looked up and my heart sank. 'Oh, hey, Stephanie.'

'What are you doing here?' Stephanie asked.

'The dining room got a little out of hand. I came here for some peace and quiet.'

Unfortunately, despite being excellent at everything else, Stephanie didn't seem to be very good at taking hints. She just nodded sympathetically and then sat down next to me. 'I've just been in the Art department.'

'Still? I thought all the Art projects had been handed in for marking already?'

'I'm doing some stuff on the side,' she shrugged.

Of course she was. It was probably a commission from the Queen or something. I wondered if that was where Connor was too.

'Anna,' she said after a few moments of silence. 'Could I talk to you about something?'

'What is it?' I asked.

'It's kind of embarrassing.' She turned her knees to face me. 'I just feel like I can talk to you.'

'That's nice,' I said.

'I like this boy.'

I snapped my neck forward so fast that I very nearly

headbutted her. She jolted backwards. 'Sorry,' I said. My stomach was churning. 'What do you mean?'

'I like this boy,' she repeated, looking down at the books she was carrying. 'And I'm not sure, but I think he likes me back.'

I felt as though all the air had been sucked out my body, like a deflated balloon discarded after a birthday party. Stephanie tucked her hair behind her ears, her cheeks turning pink. Her long eyelashes fluttered as she fiddled with the corners of her notepad.

'Do you really think he likes you back?' I had to ask it.

'Um, yes,' she smiled, still not looking at me. 'But how are you supposed to know? Maybe I should just ask him. I don't know what to do.'

'Sure,' I muttered, my heart beating so loud I could feel it in the back of my throat. 'So, what is it that makes you think he likes you exactly?'

'The way he acts. Some of the things he says – I'm not certain. But I really, really like him. Oh, I guess it's awkward for you to talk about him like this. You know . . . because of your relationship.' She looked up at me questioningly.

'My . . . relationship – no, I wouldn't call it that. It's . . . uh . . .'

'You won't tell anyone, will you?' she asked suddenly,

reaching forward and grabbing my forearm. 'Please don't.'

I shook my head, sick to my stomach. 'Of course I won't.'

'Thank you,' she sighed, leaning back on the bench. 'It's so hard to know what to do. The idea of telling someone how you feel when you're not sure if they like you back . . .' She shook her head. 'Argh! It's so nervewracking.'

'Yeah,' I whispered. 'It is.'

'But then Jess told me that Marianne had told her to go with her gut when it came to her Art project, and I thought that maybe that applied to life too.'

'Not when it comes to Cointreau,' I said quietly – but I was too sad to explain the joke when Stephanie looked at me quizzically. 'Uh, never mind. Yeah, Marianne did say that. What . . . uh . . . what does your gut say?' I wasn't sure I wanted to know the answer to my own question.

'I think I should talk to him. I should tell him how I feel.' She smiled at me. 'I've got nothing to lose, I guess.'

My eyes grew hot with tears. I tried to blink them back, hoping she might think I was squinting in the sun.

'Thanks for listening, Anna. I felt like I couldn't talk to anyone.' She hugged her notepad to her chest and then stood up. 'I'll let you be on your own now. You need to get in the zone for tomorrow. I'll be cheering for you Puffins, I don't care that I'm an Eagle.'

'Thanks,' I nodded. 'That's . . . that's really nice of you.'

I watched her walk back round to the front of the building. As soon as she had turned the corner, and I had checked there wasn't anyone lurking nearby, I burst into tears.

Hello! It's Anna here, leave a message. OK, bye!

BEEP

'Hey! It's me. Where did you go after school, ding-dong-brain? Everyone was looking for you! You can't just run off home and leave your team. And you should have seen what Danny did. Someone went, 'Yeah Puffins!' and did a loud SQUAWK. Danny turned to him and says, 'no, no, no,' – you know, all pompous – 'that's not the right sound. The cry of a puffin is much lower and subtle, almost like a growl.' And then he MADE THE SOUND. He was standing there making this weird growling sound in his throat for AGES. And the guy joined in with him! It was one of the funniest and weirdest moments of my life. And you missed out!'

Hello! It's Anna here, leave a message. OK, bye!

BEEP

'Hi, Anna, it's Danny here. Just so you know, I've been teaching everyone the call of the puffin. I think, since you're team captain, you should learn it too, so we can all do it in chorus before each race. There are some videos online, if you'd like to perfect it this evening. I'll email you the link now.'

Hello! It's Anna here, leave a message. OK, bye!

BEEP

'Hey, Anna, it's James. Where did you go after school? I was hoping to catch you before you left. Anyway, get some rest tonight because you need to be on top form tomorrow. And I know you're going to be panicking about it but, trust me on this, you'll be fine. Go team Puffin! Wow, that sounded lame. It's way better when loads of people say it together. Um, bye.'

It's Anna here, leave a message. OK, bye!

BEEP

'Hi, Anna, it's Stephanie from school, Connor gave me your number, I hope that's OK. I just wanted to say thanks for talking me today. Sorry for putting you on the spot! Hope you have a good evening and best of luck tomorrow. Go Puffins! But don't tell Sophie I said that. Bye!'

There are so many things that you can do when you're in a Hoover cupboard. Here are just some of the opportunities:

1. Try and make out the patterns of paint on the wall.

It's a lot more interesting than it sounds. Are they swirls? Did the painters create them on purpose? Do they mean something?

2. Think about how great the rest of life might be if it was a bit more like a Hoover cupboard.

No one would disturb you – you'd be left on your own.

It would be cosy and quiet. I bet that's why people move to the countryside.

3. Practice your humming.

It took time and solid dedication but I think I've finally nailed Beethoven's *Fur Elise*.

4. Practice drumming on your knees.

Now all I need is a bongo.

5. Pay attention to your loyal Labrador.

At least, until he deserts you and exits the cupboard in search of food or someone more entertaining. Traitor.

6. Plot your emigration.

I just need to master hang-gliding and I'll be Antarctica-bound.

7. Cry, because despite the fact you've done everything you can, including voluntary exercise and motivational public speaking, the boy you like more than anyone has fallen for someone else.

Of course, it would have been a lot easier to carry out these cupboard activities if my dad hadn't been banging on the door. For some reason, Dad thought that if he kept doing that I would come out. How he had got the most famous actress in the world to agree to marry him was a mystery to me.

He stood outside the Hoover cupboard door for ages giving me a pep talk about sports day and how he was really proud that I'd taken on such a challenge. Which was really sweet and everything, but wasn't enough to make me want to come out of the cupboard and have supper. At one point he went away, then there was a small tap on the bottom of the door.

'Dad. What are you doing?'

I heard a sigh. 'I was trying to waft the smell of a plate of chicken under the door. I'll leave it outside for you.'

'I'm really not hungry.'

'You will be when you've smelt this delicious chick– DOG, NO! DOG! Come back here! DOG, COME BACK HERE THIS INSTANT!'

I heard him running down the corridor. A few minutes later he was back. 'Dog ate your chicken.' He sounded disheartened.

'I'm very happy for him.'

'Anna, you've been in there for over an hour. Could you at least open the door? How about I go and get your laptop, huh? Wouldn't you like to have your laptop with you so you can email Jess?'

'Oh, sure, Dad. As soon as I open the door for you to slide in the laptop, you'll wedge your foot in after it. I know your game.'

I heard him give a long sigh and walk away down the hall again. Then I heard his low voice talking to someone on the phone. He padded back. 'I've called round some backup.'

'You called the magician?!'

'No Anna, I did not call the same magician I arranged to come to your birthday party five years ago to try and coax you out the Hoover cupboard. What made you even think about him?'

'A magician is the only thing that could cheer me up right now. You know magic blows my mind.'

'FINE. I will see if I still have his number.'

About half an hour later the doorbell rang. For a moment I really did think it was the magician but then I heard my mum, Helena, and what sounded suspiciously like Marianne's clacking heels. They all huddled round the door, making shushing noises.

'Anna?' Mum said, with a gentle knock. 'It's Mum.'

'Hi, Mum.'

'What's going on, darling? Nick says you've been in the cupboard for quite some time. He couldn't even tempt you out with some chicken.'

Great. Thanks, Dad, for making me sound like some kind of captive bear.

'Why don't you just tell us what's wrong and we'll try to help?' Marianne suggested.

'Yes, Anna, fill us in and we can work it out together,' Helena agreed.

'*Everything* is wrong.'

'Everything?' Mum repeated, sounding confused. 'Give us a list.'

'Sports day is tomorrow and I'm completely

terrified. What happens if the Puffins lose? What happens if all this training was for nothing and I'm useless? What happens if I come last in everything? What happens if I'm the worst team captain ever and everyone hates me?'

'That is very stressful,' Helena sympathised.

'But that's not the main thing. It's Connor. Or not, as the case may be.'

'Have you two broken up?' Marianne asked.

'Ah, first heartbreak! It's so tough, but we all get through it,' soothed Helena.

'We can't have broken up! We never really started dating. He has no idea how I feel about him, and now he's gone off me anyway.'

Dad cleared his throat, clearly unprepared for this sort of talk. 'Why don't you . . . uh . . . tell him how you feel, Anna?'

'Because he likes someone else now! Stephanie. She's really clever and she's artistic – and she has a very cool fringe. They're a much better match. I can't even hate her properly, she's so nice.' I sighed dramatically and buried my face in my knees. 'It's all over and it hadn't even started yet.'

'Well, what about that Jim fellow?' Dad asked.

'James? No!'

'Ooh, is he the hot guy who's been taking you out for gym sessions?' Marianne's voice brightened.

'Oh yes, he's very dishy,' Mum agreed.

'Stop, Mum! That is so disturbing.'

'I don't see why.'

'Because he's FIFTEEN YEARS OLD.'

'He seems to like you a lot,' Helena said. 'Don't you think, Nick?'

'Uh . . . yes, yes, most likely.'

'Why else would he be spending so much free time with you?' Marianne reasoned.

'He doesn't LIKE me, you weirdos! He just wants the Puffins to win sports day. And anyway, I like CONNOR!'

'Anna, don't call Helena a weirdo,' Dad scolded. 'But, got it. You like Connor, not James.'

'Oh, I see how it is,' Mum scoffed. 'So it's OK for her to call *me* a weirdo?'

'She called me one too,' Marianne sniffed.

'FINE. Anna, don't call your mother or Marianne weirdos.'

'And what about me?' Helena asked.

'Oh for goodness' sake! I already said you!'

'But then you didn't say her the second time round,' Mum pointed out. 'I can see Helena's point.'

'This is what happens when you have a family full of women!' Dad huffed.

'Don't be sexist, darling,' Helena said sternly. 'It's very unbecoming.'

Suddenly all I could think of was how ridiculous they all were. I started giggling and they went quiet. 'Anna, were you laughing? Are we cheering you up?' Mum asked eagerly.

'Yes. But you weren't doing it on purpose.'

'Oh, splendid!' Helena clapped. 'Well done us.'

'She's laughing at us, you sushi-brain! We shouldn't be happy about it,' sighed Marianne.

Helena gasped. 'Nick, aren't you going to say anything?'

'What about?'

'Marianne just called me a sushi-brain! You can't just stand there saying nothing!'

'She's your daughter. You can tell her off.'

'Technically I'll be half yours in a few months' time,' Marianne pointed out. 'So you can tell me off if you like, Nick, but only if you're not too mean about it.'

'Very well. Marianne, don't call your mother a sushi-brain.'

'Sushi-brain is an awfully good insult, isn't it?' Mum said thoughtfully.

'If it wasn't aimed at me, I'd be extremely impressed with it,' Helena agreed. 'Well done, Marianne.'

By this point my giggling had morphed into full-on laughter. I swung open the door and crawled out to look up at their faces beaming down at me.

'Hello, darling,' Mum grinned, helping me up and pulling me into a hug. 'You've come to join us.'

'Yes I have.' I smiled as Marianne reached across her to sort out my hair. 'To be honest, it's the first time in a while that I've felt like we're a family.'

Helena and Dad looked guiltily at each other.

'I know you're all really stressed at the moment,' I mumbled, anxious not to hurt anyone's feelings. 'But I've missed us all just . . .' I shrugged, 'being us, I guess.'

'Me too,' Marianne said, putting her hands on her hips. 'In fact, as we're all together, I think that this is a perfect time to talk about the wedding.'

'The wedding?' Helena glanced at Dad.

'Yes, the wedding.' Marianne threw her hands up in the air. 'The two of you are driving each other insane, not to mention the rest of us.'

'That's a little rude, darling,' Helena began. 'I appreciate we've been a bit tense, but –'

'A bit tense?' I snorted. 'Dad's hairline has gone back at least two centimetres!'

'It has not!' Dad protested, running his hand over his head.

'You've both been acting like children,' I told them.

'Oh really?' Dad's eyebrows started doing their angry wiggle. 'I don't believe it's *me* who's been in the cupboard for the last hour.'

'We're not talking about me right now,' I said, holding up my hand. 'No need for you to get defensive.' Dad looked at Mum, aghast, but she simply nodded in agreement.

'Anna's right, you need to . . .' Marianne searched for the word.

'Communicate more,' I finished for her.

'Yes, Anna, precisely,' Marianne turned to look at Helena sternly, 'communicate, Mum. You're getting too carried away. You're not listening to the people who care about you the most. At this wedding there will be no circus acts, no exploding cakes, no Big Bird dresses and no animals. Of any kind.'

'But –'

'Don't talk to me, Mum!' Marianne interrupted. 'Talk to Nick. He doesn't want a circus act or animals. Do you, Nick?'

'Uh, well.' Sighing heavily, Dad took Helena's hand in his. 'I'm sorry, Helena, I really don't want a circus act.

Or animals. Although I'm sure the Big Bird dress was actually very lovely.'

'Good,' I cut in. 'And in the future, Dad, you shouldn't react so angrily when Helena makes suggestions. Yelling is hardly going to help her see your point of view. I know you've been very stressed with the book, but Helena is your fiancée. You should put her first. Make sure she knows that she's your priority. And as a bonus, I suspect Dog will stop sitting on your glasses in protest if you calm down.'

Dad and Helena stared at me. 'Well,' Dad shook his head, a smile spreading across his face, 'looks like I've been told.'

'Looks like I've been told too,' Helena beamed at Marianne and then looked adoringly at Dad. *Gross.* 'I'm so sorry, Nick.'

'I'm sorry too, Helena.' He pulled her into a hug. I waited for an appropriate couple of seconds, enough time to share a triumphant smile with Marianne, before I pushed Dad's arm aside and joined in. Marianne did the same with Helena, and Mum joyfully wrapped her arms round all of us. Not one to be left out, Dog jumped up and clawed at my back impatiently until I broke away from the hug to push him down.

The doorbell rang. 'Ah, the final part of the backup,'

Dad announced, pulling away from Helena.

'Wait. Dad, did you really call the magician?'

'Close,' he chuckled, pulling open the front door as we all looked to see who it was.

'Hey everyone!' Jess cried as Danny, standing behind her, gave a big wave. 'Mind if we steal our team captain for a couple of hours? We've planned a little adventure for her.'

I was so happy to see them. Then I heard what Jess was planning. She appeared to have lost her mind.

'You realise that there is absolutely no way I am breaking into my own school, right?'

We were standing on the pavement by the school gate. Jess rolled her eyes. 'It's not breaking in if we go here. If anyone asks we'll say we really need a book for homework.' She put her hands on her hips authoritatively. 'Don't worry, I've got it all worked out.'

'Why don't we just call Miss Duke and check it's OK?'

'Yeah, because I've got Miss Duke on speed dial. Oh no, wait, I'm not a crazy person.'

'I don't appreciate your sarcastic tone, Jessica. Danny, you're the sensible one, you tell her. It's sports day tomorrow! If we get caught we might not be allowed to compete.'

'I'm not *always* sensible,' Danny argued.

'You are sensible a lot of the time,' Jess reminded him.

'I'm here, aren't I?'

'Very true,' Jess admitted, 'you are becoming a bit rebellious these days. Could it be because you're trying to impress someone?'

'You don't have to try and impress me, Danny,' I sighed, patting him on the shoulder. 'I know I'm a celebrity, but I won't forget you any time soon.'

Jess sniggered and Danny went red. 'Thanks, Anna.'

'Enough of this waffle,' Jess dismissed me with a wave of her hand. 'You need to see this before tomorrow. Anna, the gates are open. They haven't even locked up yet. Come on.' She started marching across the yard towards school. Danny followed her, seemingly determined to prove to us that he wasn't sensible.

I stood, shuffling my feet for a minute or so, and then I huffily jogged up to join them.

Jess started to head towards the Art building. 'Really?' I asked her. 'Jess, now is not the time for me to practice my brush strokes. When will you realise that I am not an artist?'

'I realised that when your dad showed me that pottery on your mantelpiece. That tree is just terrible.'

'It's not a tree, it's a hand.'

Jess widened her eyes at me. 'Oh!'

'Don't worry, Anna, you don't have to be an artist when you're a YouTube star,' Danny comforted me. 'Did I tell you that people have done mash-ups of the plant pot video now? There's this one guy in China who has done a whole series of them.'

'Can I go home, please?'

'No! OK, Anna,' Jess said, pointing at a window on the ground floor of the Art building that was slightly ajar. 'You first.'

I blinked at her. 'Sorry?'

'You're the smallest.'

'I am NOT the smallest.'

'I'm like ten inches taller than you!'

'That is such an exaggeration!'

'We'll give you a leg up,' Danny encouraged, pushing me closer to the window.

'Absolutely not!'

'Anna,' Jess said, sounding suddenly earnest and caring. 'It's really important to us that we do this.'

I frowned. But she was my best friend. Whatever she had planned couldn't be *that* bad, right? 'OK, then, help me up.'

'YEEEEEESS!' Jess roared, delighted. 'Get in!'

'Shhh!' Danny looked at her angrily. 'The caretaker is probably around somewhere. Let's keep it down.'

He crouched down and linked his hands together to form a sort of step. I put my hand on his shoulder and then hoisted myself up with an extra push from Jess. I grappled with the open window, reaching inside to try and get a grip on the ledge. Inwardly thanking James for making me fitter than normal this term, I pulled myself in until I was halfway through and only my legs were dangling out.

'Hang on,' I heard Jess say. 'This door is open.'

'Oh yeah!' Danny whispered excitedly. 'Cool, that's handy.'

'Guys?'

I heard footsteps and then the quiet rap of a door nudging open. 'Guys?' I whispered desperately, my legs still hanging out of the window. 'A little help?'

But they were gone, and I was stuck in a window.

Suddenly the Art room's door creaked open and a torch light shone in my face. Oh no! It must be the caretaker.

'Hey, Anna,' Danny sniggered, wiggling the torch so I could see again. 'How's it hanging?'

Jess burst out laughing and clapped him on the back. 'I was going to say that! But you delivered it way better than I could.'

'Thanks, that's really nice of you.'

'EXCUSE ME!' I attempted to squirm forward a bit more, my stomach scraping against the windowsill.

'I hate to break up this nice moment between you two, but could you give me a hand?'

'Sure, Anna, we will in a moment,' Jess said. 'You just hang in there.'

'NICE!' Danny cried, and they high-fived each other.

Note to self: get new friends.

Eventually, when they'd had their fun, they both took an arm and hauled me inside. I pulled myself up from the floor and flicked my hair with what I hoped was a Sophie-like air. 'Now, that we're here, what on earth did you want to show me?'

Jess snatched the torch from Danny and shone it under her chin so her face lit up creepily. 'Follow me, young Skywalker.'

'Jess,' I grabbed her arm and looked at Danny for confirmation. 'Did you just make a *Star Wars* reference?! Oh my goodness! You did, you did! I didn't even realise you liked those films! This is such a great revelation!! We can watch them all together! Which is your favourite episode? Oh my goodness, let's go home and have a STAR WARS MARATHON!'

Jess shook my hand off. 'Calm down, freak, I've never seen any of those loser films. You just always say that Skywalker phrase before we go in to French.'

'Oh.' I coughed and Danny pursed his lips, trying not

to laugh. 'Carry on.'

Jess led us through the room to a long row of benches at the back. They had been pulled together to exhibit all the artwork from our year group. I caught a glimpse of all the paintings and sketches as Jess ran the torchlight across them.

'Wow, are these all of the exam Art projects?'

'Yes,' Jess nodded. 'When your dad said that you were having a freak out about tomorrow, Danny and I decided that it was important for you to see this now. You need a boost of confidence to be our team captain, and we thought this would help. I wasn't going to show you until I could bring it home but,' she shrugged, 'now seems like the right time.'

She grabbed my hand and pulled me to the end of the benches, shining the torch on three huge boards propped up and clamped together. They were covered in photographs – and they were all of me. Across the top of the centre board in calligraphy was the title *The Real Deal*.

'Cool, huh?' Danny smiled, ruffling my hair. 'You look great!'

'It's an exploration of what is presented to us versus what is really there,' Jess explained. 'It's a critique of the media that's also an examination of the hidden side of a person. What makes them, them. What makes you, you, Anna.'

My eyes welled up as I took in the photographs. They were incredible. Jess had captured moments throughout the term that hadn't seemed all that important at the time. Looking back, though, I realised that they had been amazing. There were images of me in every situation: playing with Dog, hitting Danny over the head, laughing with Marianne in my Snoopy dressing gown, some photos of Jess and I that she had taken when we were lying down on the grass, one of me learning how to throw a discus, and a perfectly timed shot of me rolling my eyes, Dad blurred in the background. There was even one of me at the starting line on the sports field. James was silhouetted at the front of the picture but the focus was on me, eyes forward, ready to run, determined expression on my face.

Alongside the photographs were newspaper cuttings and website print-outs, including snippets of Tanya Briers's article, woven through the photos. My eye went from a photo of me in my uniform, throwing my arms around Danny with my eyes closed and a goofy smile on my face, to a photo of me posing in a long purple Prada dress at a premiere with the caption, *This is It: Anna Huntley (pictured) was recently attacked for being a terrible role model to young girls.*

'Jess!' I couldn't think of the words. 'Why did you –'

'Because it's important,' she said matter-of-factly. 'The media has had their say, I wanted to have mine.'

'Jess always has to have the last word,' Danny grinned, nudging her waist with his elbow.

'It's . . . well . . . it's . . .' I just smiled at her, unable to stop a tear from rolling down my cheek.

'Oh, God, don't get mushy. It was an Art project. It's not serious stuff.' She laughed as I threw myself at her, patting my back awkwardly while I clung on. 'Yes, yes.'

'We thought that this would give you a reminder that you are someone to look up to, whether you're a winning captain or not,' said Danny.

'Very nicely put, Danny,' Jess approved, gently pushing me off her to stop me getting her t-shirt damp with my tearful face.

'Sorry,' I sniffled, wiping my nose with my sleeve. 'I didn't realise that was what you were working on. Thanks for taking me here, guys. Hey!' I clutched Jess's arm excitedly. 'Can we see Connor's project? It will be here, won't it? It's finished!'

I snatched the torch from her hand and followed the spotlight across the table, waiting for it to land on *The Amazing It Girl*. But it wasn't there. 'That's weird,' I shone the light on the other benches around the room, 'maybe they put it with another year group's projects by accident? Can you guys see it anywhere?'

'Actually, uh, I don't think that one is here,' Jess said.

'Where is it?'

Jess shrugged.

My heart sank and, embarrassingly, my eyes filled with tears. Luckily, it was too dark for the others to notice. 'I'm such an idiot.' I passed the torch back to Jess. 'Of course it's not here.'

'Why are you an idiot?' Danny asked gently.

'Because I actually thought that he was still interested in *The Amazing It Girl*!' I said, exasperated. 'But why would he be? Clearly it's no longer important to him.'

'That's not true,' Jess said.

'It *is* true. Look around. It's not here. It's probably in a bin somewhere. You don't have to be nice about this, I don't know why I was silly enough to believe it might be here. Which one is Connor's project? Is it that big bumblebee painting?'

'Anna –'

My phone started ringing. 'It's Dad,' I said, shoving it back in my pocket. 'We should go.'

Jess sighed. 'Come on.'

As we crept back silently out of the school I kicked myself for daring to believe that there might still be something between me and Connor. All the effort I'd put in to sports day had been for nothing. Who cared if the Puffins won? Connor wouldn't look at me any differently. I wasn't the Amazing It Girl any more.

We got to the end of my road and I said goodbye to Danny and Jess. They each gave me pep talks about leading the Puffins to victory, and if I hadn't been feeling so sad about Connor I might have actually laughed at their movie-style speeches.

I began to walk back down my road. 'Hey, It Girl!' Jess cried behind me. I stopped and turned round. 'Not to sound like my dad,' she grinned and punched the air, 'but in the words of Bon Jovi, *keep the faith*!'

I wasn't sure if she was talking about Connor or the Puffins, but it didn't matter. I had lost confidence in both.

'Breakfast?'

Helena was standing proudly next to a kitchen table groaning under the amount of food on it. There were pastries of every kind, cured meats, about twelve different brands of yoghurt, bowls of fruit, a saucer of bacon, scrambled eggs, mushrooms, tomatoes and beans, pancakes drizzled with honey, brown and white toast, and a selection of juices.

Apparently, this is what happens when you let a movie star be in charge of breakfast.

'Is there anything that takes your fancy?' Helena asked, gesturing at the feast.

'I imagine there will be. You've obviously been to every continent to get this breakfast selection.'

'In my experience,' Helena said, sitting down and reaching for some strawberries, 'when you're nervous before an audition, you never know what will take your fancy. And you have to eat something, so I like to be prepared and just listen to my body on the day. You look splendid, my love.'

I tugged at my orange, white and black Puffin t-shirt.

'How are you feeling?' Dad asked, pulling out a chair and sitting next to Helena.

'Sick.'

'Excellent,' Helena beamed. 'You need the adrenaline. Now sit down and let's get you ready to go.'

I joined them at the table and nibbled at some toast with sliced banana on it ('for energy, darling'). I was too nervous to talk, so Dad and Helena struck up a conversation about the food dehydrator that Helena had recently purchased. I sat in silence, butterflies having some kind of big party in my stomach. If I hadn't have been feeling so terrible, I would have been even more pleased about the way Dad and Helena were acting today. They were holding hands at the table, gazing into each other's eyes and being very considerate of each other, constantly asking each other if they wanted something else. Usually I would have thrown a croissant at Dad's head at their unnecessary display of affection but today I was just relieved.

Before I knew it, Mum was at the door, holding a big banner that said GO PUFFINS! on it, and I was being ushered into the car to school. 'Marianne is meeting us there,' Helena smiled, looking round from the front seat as Mum held my hand in the back. 'She got held up by something.'

I was completely dreading the day. I kept wondering how I had managed to get myself into such an awful situation. I wished I could go back in time and say no to Jess and Danny's ridiculously stupid plan.

That was, until we pulled up to the sports field.

I couldn't believe my eyes. It was so colourful. Peering out the window, I could see all the students wearing face paint – orange, white and black stripes for Puffins, black and gold for Eagles, as well as school flags and banners pitched into the ground. There was an ice-cream van, and even (non alcoholic) drinks tents. No wonder the Puffins vs. Eagles thing was such a big deal. They really did go all out here.

I stepped out of the car to an onslaught of hugs and high-fives from my fellow Puffins. Someone even drew some Puffin stripes on to my face. James parted the crowd to get to me. 'Hey!' he said, admiring my face paint. He put his hands on my shoulders and looked at me intently. 'You ready, Captain?'

'Of course!' I lied, and James led me towards the centre of the field, leaving my parents and Helena to follow with their hampers of food. I say hampers, plural: apparently movie stars don't do normal picnics either. Helena's hampers were actually sponsored by a champagne brand.

You know you've made it when a champagne brand wants to sponsor your school sports day picnic.

They settled down with the other parents in the spectator areas at the side of the tracks while James and I went to join Danny, Jess and some other Puffins by the scoreboard. Jess squealed and gave me a massive hug when she saw me, but Danny was a little quiet. 'I'm a bit nervous,' he admitted.

'Oh, whatever.' Jess blew a raspberry at him. 'You're only doing shot put. Anna has *four* events! And she's just as bad at this kind of thing.' She laughed and then she noticed my face. 'That was the . . . uh . . . old days, though,' she coughed. 'Way back when. These days you're a sporting hero, Anna! I wouldn't be surprised to see Anna Huntley for Great Britain at the next Olympics –'

'You can stop now,' I informed her, patting her shoulder appreciatively.

The first competitors, including Danny, were being called up to the track.

Danny waved as he jogged away and Jess gave him a thumbs-up. 'I'll find you later, Anna!' he called.

James came up to me. 'You know your event order, right?' he asked, taking me aside as though he was an ACTUAL trainer. I genuinely think he forgot that we weren't in the Olympics. 'Discus first, then one hundred metre sprint, then long jump, and then relay to finish.'

'I really think I might throw up.'

'Don't do that,' he said, wrinkling up his nose at the thought. 'Let's do some stretches to warm up.'

After we'd warmed up, we went to watch some events. I wanted to keep an eye on the points, but I winced as the Eagles took an easy lead. We didn't seem to be able to come back from it either as the next round of events began. But because James still had hope, I still had hope. 'Keep smiling, Anna,' he told me, 'everyone is looking to you.'

So I stood there, grinning like a weird person on the off-chance that someone disappointed at the Puffins' score would see me smiling and feel encouraged. 'Why are you doing that creepy face?' James asked after a few minutes.

'What? I'm not! I'm smiling at everyone encouragingly!'

'You're freaking everyone out. Look determined.'

I changed my expression.

'I said, look determined, not like a villain in a Bond movie. Why are you doing that with your eyebrows?'

'I was trying to look *determined*,' I hissed at him.

Our exchange was interrupted by my name being

called for the first round of discus. I gulped and instinctively grabbed James's arm. 'Oh, no.'

'Oh yes.'

'I can't do it.'

'Yes you can.'

'I'll kill someone.'

'No you won't!'

He took my arm and dragged me towards the far corner of the field, where the discus event was being held. I groaned when I saw Helena, Mum and Dad already over there, waving wildly at me. Jess and Danny came over to offer me words of encouragement, but I couldn't listen to them. More and more saliva built up in my mouth as I waited for my turn.

'Anna, you're up next,' Miss Clifford nodded at me.

I was very temped to say, 'nope,' and just run away. But I couldn't do that, not with my entire family watching. Mum was holding up the banner, Helena was waving a Union Jack for some unknown reason, and they all applauded when I stepped forward.

I took hold of the discus, trying to ignore the fact that I'd seen at least three people take a step backwards as I did so.

I took a deep breath, like James always told me to do.

'Big, big throw, Anna!' bellowed my dad. I clutched

the discus and, aware that all eyes were on me, I swung my arm backwards with every ounce of energy I could muster and then flew it forward, releasing the discus.

As the discus soared out of my hand and into the air, I fell backwards. I landed in a starfish position staring up at the sky.

With my history of balance, it's a view I'm getting quite used to.

'Not bad.' Miss Clifford's face loomed over me as I squinted up at her. She held out a hand and pulled me to my feet. 'It may not be the world's greatest throw, but if we were grading it, I'd give you an A* for effort.'

I looked out to see my throw being marked by another sports teacher. She came back to report my distance to Miss Clifford. 'Well?' I asked eagerly as she noted it down.

'I can't tell you the results, Anna,' she said sternly, clutching her clipboard to her chest. I tried my best impression of Dog's please-give-me-some-bacon-I-love-you face. 'Oh, all right. You didn't come last, OK?'

My jaw dropped. *I didn't come last?* I DIDN'T COME LAST!

AND I HADN'T KILLED ANYONE WITH A DISCUS!

This was truly a glorious day.

When I reported the good news, Mum gave me a hug so tight I thought my ribs might collapse and Helena put a hand on her heart and closed her eyes with such an intense, dramatic inhale that we all instinctively fell silent and waited for her to speak. 'Simply wonderful,' she whispered.

Wow, those Oscars sure were well-deserved.

Even James seemed impressed with me – for about two seconds, until he decided to get bossy again. 'We need to go get ready for your one hundred metres.'

'Try not to fall over during this one,' Jess grinned.

'I think she actually does have a problem,' Danny informed Stephanie, who had come over to stand next to us. She looked suitably impressed. 'Some sort of internal imbalance.'

'You should do yoga,' Stephanie suggested. 'It might help you fall over less.'

I wondered how to stop Stephanie hanging out with us.

James ushered me away from my group of so-called friends. 'Sorry,' he apologised. 'I don't mean to be a killjoy, but your track event is soon. You'll have more of a break between that and the long jump. You ready to go?'

I nodded and then shook my head. 'Can't I stop now that I haven't come last in discus?'

He rolled his eyes and sternly pointed at the starting line. Next to us, the crowd erupted into cheers at the heat before mine crossed the finishing line. 'Go to your lane now, Captain.'

I reluctantly made my way past the spectators and towards the starting line. I could see that Mum was waiting for me at the finish line. Her banner was waving about wildly, no doubt bashing any nearby Eagle supporters.

The starting pistol went off. I raced as fast as my legs could carry me. It was over in seconds, and as I bent double trying to catch my breath, I could hear my family cheering close by.

I felt a hard whack on the back. 'OW!' I yelped, looking up to see James next to me. 'What was that for?'

'You came fourth!' James laughed, putting both hands on my shoulders and giving me an excited shake.

'I came fourth?'

'Yes!'

'I came *fourth*? Out of *six people*?'

'Yes!'

'I am on a *roll*. That's the second time I wasn't last!'

'Unlike your team,' a familiar voice interrupted us.

'Brendan,' James said, rolling his eyes in exasperation at his friend.

'Hey, Tyndale,' Brendan smirked. 'You prepared for me to kick your butt in the sprint later . . . just like always?'

'I wouldn't be too cocky, actually, Dakers,' James replied with a sly smile. 'I've seen your recent times. I've been beating you.'

Brendan's smirk wavered ever so slightly. 'No way.'

'Ask Miss Clifford if you like,' James shrugged. 'I've been doing practice runs a lot while I was helping out Anna. She's been timing me.'

'That's right.' I nodded as Brendan looked taken aback. 'He's really fast and his timings keep improving. Miss Clifford said that he's probably the fastest in the year now.'

'Miss Clifford said that?' Brendan was shocked. Then he snorted, attempting to cover up his reaction. 'Well, I guess we'll see on the track.'

'I guess we will,' James said, patting him patronisingly on the head before leading me away from him.

'Do you think he'll actually ask Miss Clifford?' I queried.

'No, he definitely believed us,' James said, looking victorious.

'I believe us too, you know,' I pointed out. 'You can beat him.'

'Thanks, Captain.'

Next up was my long jump. Miraculously I wasn't disqualified. I landed in the way that James had taught me, sand spraying up on either side of me. 'It's in my eye!'

I cried. Then I crawled out of the pit on all fours, my eye weeping as I crouched on the grass.

Jess came over to get me to my feet. She used the back of her hand to wipe a sandy tear off my cheek and took a step back to survey my face. 'You look really good right now.'

I tried to whack her, but because there was still sand in my eye I missed.

'I can't get over it!' Dad was saying to Mum and Helena as we joined them where they'd set up their picnic, once I could see properly again. 'It just shows what you can do when you put your mind to it. Anna, why do you look like you've been stung by a bee?'

'Thanks for that, Dad. Way to motivate me,' I grumbled. 'I fell in the sand. More importantly, though, how are the Puffins doing?'

The faces around me dropped. 'That bad?' I groaned, peering around them to look at the scoreboard. 'How is this possible?'

'They have some very strong team members,' Helena admitted. 'They just seem to keep coming first.'

I looked round and realised that all the energy had gone from the Puffin team. Everyone was sitting around gloomily watching the scoreboard or making their way to their events with glum expressions. Even the ice cream van queue was only Eagles.

'It's not that bad!' I argued, pointing at the board. 'We can definitely catch up. We're only halfway through, right?'

'You have a point,' said James, nodding at me. 'What you need to do is get that message to everyone else.'

'How?' I bit my lip. It just seemed impossible.

But then the answer to our troubles hit us in the form of Marianne Montaine. Suddenly the whole field's attention turned. Eyes widened and jaws dropped.

Marianne had come as a Puffin.

She was wearing the puffin costume.

Marianne Montaine, It Girl and famous socialite, was wearing the full-on puffin costume. *My* puffin costume. Accompanied, no less, by an entourage: Tom Kyzer, lead singer of On The Rox, wearing a Puffin t-shirt with his usual leather skinny trousers and some woman I had never seen before.

'What the –'

'Sorry we're late! We got a bit held up, I didn't realise how difficult it was to get into this thing,' cried Marianne, peering out from under the beak. 'Plus we had to pick up Tanya on the way.' She gestured at the woman holding the notepad, who gave me a small wave of greeting.

'That's *Tanya Briers*?'

'I wanted to show her what real It Girls get up to.'

'Marianne has given me an exclusive on you as team captain here at Woodfield.' Tanya quickly looked at my dad, whose jaw had clenched. 'As long as that's OK with you, Mr Huntley, and with the headmistress of Woodfield, of course.'

'It'll be fine,' Marianne dismissed.

'Anna, how are us Puffins doing?' Tom asked. It was really very sweet of him. I'm sure an Eagle would have fitted his band image a lot more.

'We're losing,' I said, quietly. 'But now that we have an It Girl and a rock star on our side . . .'

'*Two* It Girls,' Marianne corrected, bashing me with her wing. 'Right then, let's get going.'

She waddled past me and began to flap her wings. 'PU-FFINS! PU-FFINS! PU-FFINS!'

Tom Kyzer went to stand next to her. Holding his arms up in the air as though he were on stage at a rock festival addressing all his fans, he joined in. 'PU-FFINS! PU-FFINS!'

The whole field erupted into cheers. It felt like the beginning of the day again.

It was a sports day Puffin miracle.

The next round of events began and there was a new surge of energy. Puffins were clapping each other on the back and spurring each other on. I practically lost my voice I was cheering so hard.

As team captain, I tried to make my way round as many events as possible, with Marianne plodding along as a mascot. Tanya Briers was also eagerly following, jotting down every moment.

And slowly, bit by bit, the Puffins started to draw closer to the Eagles' score line.

With only a few races remaining, James stepped up to the starting line for his heat alongside Brendan. The two boys eyed each other up warily.

The bang of the starting gun echoed around the field and they shot off. It was incredibly close, but as they came stampeding across the finish line, James sailed through with Brendan just behind him.

He was beaming. 'Anna, I did it!' I didn't even hesitate. I ducked under the rope separating the spectators from the track and ran over to give him a hug.

I wish I had hesitated, though, because he was really sweaty.

Brendan gave him a grudging clap on the back and James turned to me with the most enormous grin. 'I did it, Team Captain. I won! Your turn next.'

'You'll be fine,' Jess comforted me as we left our families on the picnic rug to make our way to the relay track for the last event. 'Just don't drop the baton like you usually do, because then we'll lose everything.'

'Thanks. You are so helpful.'

'You've got this!' Stephanie called after us.

'She *is* lovely,' Jess commented.

'Hmmm . . . have you seen Connor anywhere? I haven't seen him all day.'

'Glimpses of him,' Jess answered, cracking her knuckles. 'He's here somewhere. He'll be watching.'

But I couldn't see him anywhere. Jess pinched me hard on the arm. 'I need your full focus, Anna.'

'Yeah, you're right. I'm focused.'

'The Puffins will actually win sports day if we win this race!'

'Yeah,' I gulped. 'But I have to cross that finishing line. And I'm up against Sophie.'

'Just focus on your own run. Don't worry about Sophie running next to you,' Jess waggled her finger at me. 'And, whatever you do . . .'

'Don't drop the baton.'

'It will be fine! Just take the baton from me when I pass it to you.'

'Well, don't make it too sweaty with your hand.'

'I don't make it too sweaty! It's because your hands are all sweaty from your nerves that you keep dropping it. You won't this time, I know it.' She smiled, gave me a knock on the shoulder and then headed over to her starting area.

James came up to me as I stood rigidly at my line,

my mouth suddenly so dry that I couldn't even swallow. 'You've got this, Anna,' he said with a smile.

'Actually, I don't think I have,' I croaked.

'You're on fire today.'

'There's a lot more pressure on this one. Everyone's watching.'

'Don't think about any of that.'

'I feel faint. And sick. And hot. And cold. And shaky. Maybe I have pneumonia! I should go and tell Miss Duke that I have pneumonia so I can't run the race.' I looked around me desperately. 'Miss Duke! Miss Duke! Pneumonia!'

'Anna, stop randomly yelling "pneumonia".' James steadied me with his hands on my shoulders. 'Breathe.'

He took a really deep breath and I followed suit. We exhaled together. 'Better?' he asked after we'd repeated the deep breathing a few times.

I nodded. 'Good luck,' he said simply before he left me on my own and jogged confidently over to the other side of the track. He was running the starting leg of the relay.

When he got there, he held the red baton up towards me proudly. I gave him a weak thumbs-up and tried to focus on not throwing up as Sophie took her place next to me.

That was when I saw Connor.

He was standing right up at the rope, directly in my eyeline as I looked past Sophie.

And he smiled at me.

He smiled. WHAT DID THAT MEAN?!

Wait, where was he going? He was turning round. He was moving through the crowd, away from the track. Why would he do that when he had a front row position?! I craned my neck, desperately trying not to lose sight of him. Was he going towards the finish line? Had he come to the front of the start just to smile at me?

WHY DID I NOT KNOW ANY OF THESE ANSWERS?!

I was so distracted by the back of Connor's head that I barely noticed that the crowd had suddenly quietened down and Miss Duke was raising the pistol high above her head. I took a very, very, VERY deep breath. Then the shot fired and the crowd exploded.

I watched James speed through his leg and pass the baton to the second Puffin. They actually inched ahead of the Eagle as they passed the baton to Jess. Oh no. I was up next. WHY HAD I DONE THIS TO MYSELF?!

Wait, was I actually going to throw up? No, I couldn't throw up, not in front of all these people. Not in front of Connor. WHAT IF I THREW UP IN FRONT OF CONNOR?!

Anna, I heard James scold in my head, just like he had in the baton-passing practices. When I kept DROPPING it. *Focus on Jess. She's coming your way.*

I saw Jess hit the first marker and I started running. Then I heard her yell, 'HAND!'

I reached back, I felt the baton in my hand, I gripped it tight, I saw Sophie look back in the corner of my vision, but I kept my eyes forward and I just ran, ran, ran.

The reason we won was because of Connor Lawrence.

And, OK, maybe also because the other three members of my team happened to be super speedy and gave me a good head start which was pretty handy, considering that I brought the average pace of our team down considerably.

It was super close between Sophie and me. She's so fast that even with my team's lead it wasn't too difficult for her to catch up with a slowcoach like me. But I had realised that I needed to speak to Connor so badly that there was no way I was letting him out of my sight, and so I ran harder than I ever had before.

I felt the finish-line rope, that I had never managed to touch before, hit my waist and come loose. I tumbled on to the ground and hardly had time to breathe when I felt a strong pair of arms wrap round my waist and lift me up into the air triumphantly.

'Anna, you did it!' James yelled, holding me up for everyone to see as they all crowded round. 'We won!'

And we had. And it was amazing – but scanning the crowd from above James's head I realised that the one person I wanted to be there – the person who I had run for – wasn't. And I needed to fix that.

'James.' He lowered me and leaned down to hear what I had to say above all the cheering.

'I need you to do me a favour.'

I found him in the car park, leaning into the back of a car.

'Connor.'

He jumped so high that he hit his head on the car door.

'Sorry!' I said hurriedly, as Connor shuffled backwards, rubbing the top of his head.

'No, no, I just wasn't . . .' He looked at me curiously. 'Aren't you meant to be lifting a certain trophy right now?'

I was just about to explain when there was a huge cheer from the main field. 'James stepped in at the last minute. I wanted to come see you.'

'Anna,' Connor furrowed his eyebrows in worry, 'why would you do that?'

'James is much more worthy of holding up that trophy than I am. I told him to tell everyone that I wasn't feeling well.'

'But you've worked so hard. This is your crowning moment of glory.'

'Yeah, well, I realised that I don't really care about it.'

I stopped and took a deep breath. 'I kind of care about something else.'

Connor looked at me so intently that I thought I was going to fall over again.

He didn't say anything, just reached back into the car and pulled out a thin white envelope. 'I was going to bring this over to you later. Obviously, I wanted you to enjoy your moment of victory and wasn't expecting you to . . . well, anyway. Here.' He held it out.

'What is it?' I asked, reaching out to take it from him and noticing a LOT that our fingers brushed as I did. It had already been opened and the beautifully-written address on the front was his. I pulled the folded letter out and opened it up.

'Read it,' he instructed.

'"Dear Mr Lawrence,"' I began, '"we are delighted to announce that you are the winner of the Graphic Novel Association UK's Young Adult Comic Book Competition."'

I jolted my head up. 'Keep reading,' Connor grinned, putting his hands in his pockets.

'"Your entry, *The Amazing It Girl* –"' I hesitated. 'Connor . . .'

'Keep reading,' he insisted.

'"Your entry, *The Amazing It Girl*, was the clear winner for all of our judges who thought it outstanding in both design and plot. As the winner of our national competition, you are invited to visit world-famous graphic novel studio, Caption, to witness first-hand how a comic book comes together. Caption is also thrilled to be able to publish *The Amazing It Girl* as a comic book in its own right. Many congratulations, and please do get in touch so we can discuss your well-deserved win in detail."'

I finished reading, folded the letter up and slipped it back into its envelope.

Connor reached into the car again and this time pulled out a comic book, handing it to me.

It was *The Amazing It Girl*. A real published book that anyone could buy or read. I turned it over in my hands and opened it to admire the glossy pages. I couldn't believe he'd done this for me.

'Why?'

'It's what I wanted the world to see, Spidey. After that viral video, everyone had it so wrong. I wanted them all to know the real you.' Connor blushed. 'The *amazing* you.'

'That's cheesy even for you, Lawrence,' I laughed.

'I know,' he grinned. 'But I had to turn my sketches into something bigger to be able to show people what I could see – not what the newspapers were saying. I'd actually seen this competition a while back, and didn't think I was good enough to enter, but then when everything happened, I showed Stephanie and she said that I definitely should.'

But something was niggling me. 'Connor, I've hardly seen you all term . . .'

'I know,' he nodded. 'I didn't expect to win. But then when I found out I had, just when everything went crazy after the press conference, I didn't want you to think that this book was me jumping on that bandwagon and hoping to get publicity for it. So I tried to back off until it all blew over. It was hard because . . . you know . . . I kind of missed you, but every time we got . . . uh . . . close, something seemed to get in the way.' His words all tumbled out and he blushed.

'Yeah,' I said, equally embarrassed. He was talking about *kissing*. Us kissing. Me and Connor. 'Sorry about that. I'm going to blame Dog for at least one of those incidents.'

Connor laughed. 'So, do you like it?' he asked nervously, chewing his lip. 'The book, I mean. Let me know what you think.'

So I did.

27

I kissed a boy.

I KISSED A BOY!

A BOY!

And not just any old boy. But Connor! Connor, who is a boy!

See you later, Mr Albatross. Antarctica might just be off the cards.

That evening, Connor was outside my door at 7.30 on the dot. As he stood there, his dark eyes peeking out from under his scruffy fringe and that mischievous grin on his face, I practically melted at the memory of stepping towards him as he leaned in and, without any hindrance from doors or dogs, pulled me into the most amazing kiss.

'Never thought I'd say this, but, ready to go to Brendan's?' he asked.

Brendan Dakers, no doubt expecting an easy Eagle win, had, earlier in the term, invited the entire year group to his house for a big party the evening of sports day. It was nice of him to include everyone – I can't imagine Sophie and Josie had been too happy about that. 'I bet Brendan's mum told him he had to,' Jess had suggested.

'Bye, Mum! Bye, Dad! Bye, Helena! Bye, Marianne!' I went to quickly shut the door behind me but before I could there was a stampede. Suddenly my family and Dog were filling up the hallway.

'Hey there, buddy,' Connor crouched down to Dog, who ran full speed at him. In his excitement he forgot to stop and headbutted Connor's knees.

'Connor, we didn't realise you had arrived!' Mum said in an excited tone, beaming at him.

'Yeah, well, we're off now. Come on, Dog,' I gently tugged at his collar and handed him to Mum. 'Bye, everyone.'

'Not so fast, Anna!' Dad growled. I shot a warning look at Connor but he was hiding his smirk VERY well. 'If you make me wait when I come to pick you up . . .'

'Dad, there's no chance that I'm going to risk you coming into the party and sparking up a conversation about rotating gun turnips with the nearest teenager.'

'Turrets, Anna! Not turnips, turrets. I thought you were listening when we had that conversation. You looked so interested!'

'Got to go, bye!'

'Ah,' we heard Helena sigh as Connor and I walked down the steps and towards his mum's car, 'young love. Look how it blossoms.'

Connor pursed his lips, trying desperately not to laugh.

I wondered whether Dog would be able to come with me when I moved to Antarctica.

When we arrived at Brendan's, Jess pretended that she was just hanging out on her own by the door, but I knew she was waiting for Connor and me to show up together. She gave me a big hug and coyly said hi to Connor. 'I'll go get us some drinks,' Connor said, going over to where Brendan's mum had set up a huge table of food and drinks for everyone.

Once he had gone, Jess dragged me down to a weird hut thing at the end of the garden path. 'So, WHAT WAS IT LIKE?'

I couldn't help laughing at how excited she was. 'I don't know how to explain it!'

'Try,' she demanded.

'The best thing ever?'

'I can't believe how sneaky you were, off kissing a boy while we were celebrating!'

'It was pretty awesome,' I grinned.

'So, is Connor your boyfriend now?'

'I don't know, I didn't ask.' I sat up straight. 'Do you think I should have asked? What happens if he doesn't want to be my boyfriend?! Do you think he does?'

'Relax, you big freakface,' Jess chuckled. 'I'm pretty sure that all of the kissing means that he wants to be your boyfriend. All that fuss for nothing eh? He liked you the whole time. You know, he told me about the book a couple of days ago, but he asked me not to mention it to you.'

'He did a pretty amazing thing for me,' I swooned.

'You've done some pretty amazing things too. The Puffins won today thanks to you.'

'Thanks to *everyone* on the Puffin team, more like. Especially James.'

'He's been asking after you.'

'Who? James?'

'Yes, dumb-dumb, James. He asked what time you were coming. Hey, look,' she nudged me in the ribs and pointed down the garden. 'Do you think he's asking her out on a date?'

She seemed to be pointing to where Danny and Stephanie were sitting together and chatting on a picnic blanket on the lawn, right beneath a tree with its branches wrapped in fairy lights. I tried to see who was behind them, but I couldn't see anyone.

'Who are you looking at?' I asked, confused.

'Danny, you doofus.'

'Danny?' I scoffed. 'Why would he be asking Stephanie out on a date?'

'Oh, I don't know, maybe because they fancy the pants off each other?'

I turned to look at her. 'Huh?'

'Are you kidding? You haven't noticed? All this sports day malarkey has really been distracting you from using your brain cells.' She rapped me on the head. 'Stephanie and Danny? They're all, you know,' she made a face, 'goo-goo-eyed about each other.'

'Stephanie and Danny? STEPHANIE AND DANNY?!'

'All right, keep your voice down. What's wrong with you? Everyone knows about it. You are so late to the party. Why do you think she's been hanging around so much? Oh, wait,' her eyes widened in understanding. 'Did you still think she was into Connor?'

I nodded slowly.

'Oh, yeah, you were so wrong about that,' she chuckled. 'It was Danny who she had her eye on the whole time. I noticed that a while back.'

'And you didn't think to tell me?' I whacked her round the head.

Bad move. She whacked me right back and then we started grappling.

Someone coughed.

We both snapped our heads up to see James Tyndale standing there with a bemused expression. 'Sorry to disturb you.'

'Not disturbing at all!' I smiled, happy. We hadn't seen each other since the trophy ceremony.

'I wanted to say congratulations to our captain,' he said.

'Well, I'm going to go say hi to Danny. He's been ignoring me all evening,' Jess announced, standing up. 'You can take my place.'

James shuffled over to sit next to me and gave me a happy nudge. 'You did me proud, Team Captain, you did me proud.'

'It's all thanks to you, you know,' I began. 'I'm really happy that you made the decision to train me up this term. Today could have been *very* different if you hadn't.'

'It's been fun. Really fun.' He glanced up and nodded to where Connor, carrying our drinks, had sat down on the blanket with Stephanie, Danny and Jess. I could see him studying James carefully. 'So I heard you came here with Lawrence?'

'Yeah,' I blushed. 'He asked me.'

'So we both got what we wanted from this,' he said,

leaning forward and resting his arms on his legs. 'Well, that's great.'

There was a weird silence, and then James took a deep breath and sat up, seeming a bit more like himself. 'So, the summer trip. Are you going?'

'What's that?'

'School trip this summer. Didn't you see the notice on the board? Everyone's talking about it.'

'Everyone's been talking about sports day, I think you'll find,' I corrected him pompously.

'You should come,' he said. 'Get Jess and that lot to sign up too. It will be fun.'

'OK, I'll pitch it to them.'

'Good,' he nodded, looking at me. 'I'd like you to come.'

'Tyndale!' Brendan's voice carried across the garden from where he was standing on the patio, surrounded, as ever, by a huge group of people all craning to get his attention. 'Since you've already beaten me once today, I'm challenging you to some hardcore table football. Then we'll see who the true champion is.'

James gave me a smile and then stood up and headed towards the house where he was greeted with loud cheers. I got up too, and happily went to join my friends on the picnic blanket.

'Here,' Connor said, passing me a cup and giving me a

kiss on the cheek. In front of EVERYONE.

I was so happy that nothing could have spoiled that perfect moment – even when I spilled my entire drink down myself.

And Jess laughed. Quite a lot.

Anyway, it was just perfect.

WORLD EXCLUSIVE: IT GIRL ANNA TRIUMPHS!

British It Girl Anna Huntley led her school team to a spectacular victory this weekend. **Tanya Briers** talks to her family, friends, teachers and Anna herself to discover just why she is fast becoming the perfect role model for a new generation. Turn to page 2 for more!

From: anna_huntley@zingmail.co.uk
To: marianne@montaines.co.uk; rebecca.blythe@
bouncemail.co.uk; helena@montaines.co.uk
Subject: THE PLAN

OK, team, I have come up with the BEST prank to play on Dad. He's been really stressed recently, as you know, and I think it would be really fun to remind him to laugh at himself.

AVENGERS ASSEMBLE!

Who's in?

Love, me xxx

From: helena@montaines.co.uk
To: marianne@montaines.co.uk; rebecca.blythe@
bouncemail.co.uk; anna_huntley@zingmail.co.uk

Subject: Re: THE PLAN

Oh, how exciting! I'm in!

Except I'm not quite sure what we're avenging?

Helena x

From: marianne@montaines.co.uk
To: rebecca.blythe@bouncemail.co.uk; anna_
huntley@zingmail.co.uk; helena@montaines.co.uk
Subject: Re: THE PLAN

Pranks are classic. I'm absolutely in. Mum, remember that time I played that hilarious prank on that horrible tutor you hired? Haha!

Are we avenging the fact that Nick made us watch that boring running film the other day?

Marianne x

From: helena@montaines.co.uk
To: marianne@montaines.co.uk; rebecca.blythe@
bouncemail.co.uk; anna_huntley@zingmail.co.uk

Subject: Re: THE PLAN

Yes, Marianne, I do remember that prank you played on that highly-recommended, highly-qualified tutor I hired.

You shouldn't be proud of yourself for that, you know. She had custard in her hair for days.

The hairdresser's bill was quite something.

Helena x

From: rebecca.blythe@bouncemail.co.uk
To: marianne@montaines.co.uk; anna_huntley@
zingmail.co.uk; helena@montaines.co.uk
Subject: Re: THE PLAN

Great idea, Anna darling! I can't think of anyone better to do a prank on than Nick, he needs to have a bit of fun.

Are we pouring custard over his head? Fantastic!

Rebecca x

From: anna_huntley@zingmail.co.uk

**To: marianne@montaines.co.uk; rebecca.blythe@
bouncemail.co.uk; helena@montaines.co.uk
Subject: Re: THE PLAN**

No. We are not pouring custard over his head. That's lame.

And we're not avenging anything. I just put that in because
it's a very famous catchphrase of Marvel's Avengers. We're
a team, like they are? You know? It's really, really famous?

Never mind.

And, just to confirm, Marianne, that was ME who chose
'that boring running film', *Chariots of Fire*. I put it on so
you could see the internal struggle that athletes like Eric
Liddell and myself have to face.

Now, back to the prank. Just to check before I go ahead –
Helena, do you still have the phone number of that circus
act you tried to book for the wedding?

Love, me xxx

**From: marianne@montaines.co.uk
To: rebecca.blythe@bouncemail.co.uk; anna_**

huntley@zingmail.co.uk; helena@montaines.co.uk
Subject: Re: THE PLAN

Wait just one second. Pouring custard over someone's head is not lame. It took a huge amount of skill, timing and precision to achieve.

I'm not sure I want to take part in this prank now that you've been so rude about mine.

Good day.

Marianne x

From: anna_huntley@zingmail.co.uk
**To: marianne@montaines.co.uk; rebecca.blythe@
bouncemail.co.uk; helena@montaines.co.uk**
Subject: Re: THE PLAN

FINE, pouring custard over someone's head is a great prank.

Now will you be a part of this one?

Love, me xxx

From: marianne@montaines.co.uk
To: rebecca.blythe@bouncemail.co.uk; anna_
huntley@zingmail.co.uk; helena@montaines.co.uk
Subject: Re: THE PLAN

Say it like you mean it.

Marianne x

From: helena@montaines.co.uk
To: marianne@montaines.co.uk; rebecca.blythe@
bouncemail.co.uk; anna_huntley@zingmail.co.uk
Subject: Re: THE PLAN

Why do you need the phone number of the circus act,
Anna? Are you planning on booking them for a school
event?

I think it's simply wonderful how involved with school you
are. I wish Marianne had been so attentive to her studies!

Helena x

From: rebecca.blythe@bouncemail.co.uk

To: marianne@montaines.co.uk; anna_huntley@ zingmail.co.uk; helena@montaines.co.uk
Subject: Re: THE PLAN

It is wonderful, isn't it, Helena? I think she gets that from me. I was always very focused and driven at school.

Rebecca x

From: helena@montaines.co.uk
To: marianne@montaines.co.uk; rebecca.blythe@ bouncemail.co.uk; anna_huntley@zingmail.co.uk
Subject: Re: THE PLAN

I can well believe that, Rebecca! I was also very ambitious and, once I got into drama school, I worked extremely hard every day.

My physical theatre teacher once told me he'd never seen such motivation. Nor such an elegant neck.

Helena x

From: rebecca.blythe@bouncemail.co.uk
To: marianne@montaines.co.uk; anna_huntley@

zingmail.co.uk; helena@montaines.co.uk

Subject: Re: THE PLAN

Now that I think of it, you really do have an elegant neck,
Helena!

Rebecca x

From: anna_huntley@zingmail.co.uk
To: marianne@montaines.co.uk; rebecca.blythe@
bouncemail.co.uk; helena@montaines.co.uk
Subject: Re: THE PLAN

Can we FOCUS, please?

Helena, I am not trying to book the circus act for an event
at school. It's for the PRANK.

I need to ask them if we can borrow a couple of their
clowns and maybe a gymnast.

Love, me xxx

From: rebecca.blythe@bouncemail.co.uk
To: marianne@montaines.co.uk; anna_huntley@

zingmail.co.uk; helena@montaines.co.uk
Subject: Re: THE PLAN

How marvellous, Anna!

Do we need the gymnast to somehow climb up on top of a door and set up the custard so it falls on his head? Good thinking!

Rebecca x

From: marianne@montaines.co.uk
To: rebecca.blythe@bouncemail.co.uk; anna_huntley@zingmail.co.uk; helena@montaines.co.uk
Subject: Re: THE PLAN

Oh, I see how it is. You call my prank lame and then you just go and steal the idea.

Marianne x

From: helena@montaines.co.uk
To: marianne@montaines.co.uk; rebecca.blythe@bouncemail.co.uk; anna_huntley@zingmail.co.uk
Subject: Re: THE PLAN

How funny! I'm sure they would lend us a gymnast to climb on top of a door and set up custard so it falls on his head!

I'll go give them a call now.

Helena x

From: anna_huntley@zingmail.co.uk
To: marianne@montaines.co.uk; rebecca.blythe@
bouncemail.co.uk; helena@montaines.co.uk
Subject: Re: THE PLAN

WHY IS NO ONE LISTENING TO ME!

No, Helena, do not go give them a call! My prank is WAY better than a stupid custard prank!

Helena? Can you confirm that you haven't called?

Love, me xxx

From: marianne@montaines.co.uk
To: rebecca.blythe@bouncemail.co.uk; anna_
huntley@zingmail.co.uk; helena@montaines.co.uk

Subject: Re: THE PLAN

There you go again, dissing my custard prank right in front of me when I'm a member of your team.

I don't know how the Puffins won sports day. You don't seem to have very good leadership skills.

Marianne x

From: rebecca.blythe@bouncemail.co.uk
To: marianne@montaines.co.uk; anna_huntley@ zingmail.co.uk; helena@montaines.co.uk
Subject: Re: THE PLAN

Actually Marianne, she's never been a *natural* when it comes to leadership skills.

When she was four years old, at primary school, the teacher asked Anna if she would like to lead the sing-song session, and she was so distressed that she shoved a rubber up her nose.

Rebecca x

From: marianne@montaines.co.uk
To: rebecca.blythe@bouncemail.co.uk; anna_
huntley@zingmail.co.uk; helena@montaines.co.uk
Subject: Re: THE PLAN

I don't know about you, Anna, but that story has completely made my day.

Marianne x

From: anna_huntley@zingmail.co.uk
To: marianne@montaines.co.uk; rebecca.blythe@
bouncemail.co.uk; helena@montaines.co.uk
Subject: Re: THE PLAN

MUM. Never repeat that story again.

Love, me xxx

From: helena@montaines.co.uk
To: marianne@montaines.co.uk; rebecca.blythe@
bouncemail.co.uk; anna_huntley@zingmail.co.uk
Subject: Re: THE PLAN

Good news everyone! The gymnast is willing to climb up on

top of the door and plant a pot of custard on it for when Nick comes home!

And I've just messaged Nick to tell him to get ready for a hilarious prank!

I'm really very excited. Maybe Nick will become a YouTube star too, just like you, Anna!

Helena x

From: rebecca.blythe@bouncemail.co.uk
To: marianne@montaines.co.uk; anna_huntley@ zingmail.co.uk; helena@montaines.co.uk
Subject: Re: THE PLAN

Wonderful! You are clever, Helena!

Avengers Are Go! Was that the right phrase, Anna?

Rebecca x

From: marianne@montaines.co.uk
To: rebecca.blythe@bouncemail.co.uk; anna_ huntley@zingmail.co.uk; helena@montaines.co.uk

Subject: Re: THE PLAN

Mum, you're not really supposed to tell the person you're playing a prank on that you're going to play a prank on him.

No, Rebecca, that's the Thunderbirds catchphrase. It's Avengers At The Ready or something lame like that.

Marianne x

From: rebecca.blythe@bouncemail.co.uk
To: marianne@montaines.co.uk; anna_huntley@ zingmail.co.uk; helena@montaines.co.uk
Subject: Re: THE PLAN

Thank you, Marianne. Anna does get very upset about these Martin things when people get them wrong!

Anna, we're all very excited about the custard prank - well done you!

Avengers At The Ready!

Rebecca x

From: anna_huntley@zingmail.co.uk
To: marianne@montaines.co.uk; rebecca.blythe@
bouncemail.co.uk; helena@montaines.co.uk
Subject: NEVER MIND

You should all know that I'm saving these emails for a
new book I'm writing entitled *My Family and Me: a Life of
Torture*.

Love, me xxx

From: helena@montaines.co.uk
To: marianne@montaines.co.uk; rebecca.blythe@
bouncemail.co.uk; anna_huntley@zingmail.co.uk
Subject: Re: NEVER MIND

Darling, you never said you were writing a book! How
wonderful!

Helena x

Things that I am good at

Re-compiled with (unwelcome) commentary

by Jess Delby

1. My simply uncanny duck impression

Go on then

Go on then what?

Let's see this world-famous duck impression.

No.

Why not?

It needs to be perfected.

It's a DUCK IMPRESSION. Not a Beethoven concerto. Let's see it!

Fine!

Good. OK, I see how you . . . what the –

There. What do you think?

I'm not sure whether I should be impressed or freaked out.

Let's move on while you make up your mind.

2. I can (almost) teach dogs tricks

No way. You are NOT counting that.

Dog did the trick!

He did NOT do it.

He raised his paw when I said 'paw'! That counts!

He raised his BACK PAW so that he could PEE on a lamp post.

I didn't specify which paw.

It doesn't count.

3. I am good at being sarcastic.

I can agree with this one

Thank you.

You're amazing at it.

Thanks.

Absolutely incredible.

Thank you.

Too good to be true.

Thank you very much.

The best EVER. OF ALL TIME.

Thank you, Jess.

The whole world should bow down to you and your sarcasm.

Do you want me to say that you're good at it too?
You are.

Seriously, I was wondering how long I

was going to have to keep going for. I was running out of adjectives.

4. I am good at showing boys how I feel about them.

Is this code for 'kissing'?

WHAT? No!

It is totally code for 'kissing'!

No, it's not! I mean, being . . . open with someone.

How do you even know you're good at kissing?

What? Why would you say that?

I mean, how do you know you're good at it?

I don't know! Do you think I'd be bad at it?

I'll pop a message to Connor and ask him.

DO NOT DO THAT!

It will take me one second.

PUT YOUR PHONE DOWN!

I'll only be a moment.

JESS DELBY! GIVE ME YOUR PHONE!

'Hi, Connor, so we were wondering . . .'

STOP!!! STOP!!!

Calm down, dodohead, I was only joking.

I think I just suffered a minor heart attack.

Let's move on, I'm bored of this point now.

I need to wait for my heart rate to slow down.

Geez, take your time. I thought you were an athlete.

5. I am good at not coming last all the time.

This is kind of an embarrassing one, really.

A little bit.

Not sure why you put this in writing.

Me neither.

Not really a good one to finish on.

Yeah, I kind of regret it now.

We'll have to add another one in.

I can't. I don't have anything else that I'm good at.

Don't worry, I'll write the last one.

NO.

Why not?

Because you always write something stupid and ruin the list.

That's just mean. Without my commentary, these lists would be even more boring than that film you made me watch with all the bats and that man.

BATMAN?!

Whatever, be a good friend and let me write the last point.

Fine.

OK. Here you go, the last point on Anna Huntley's list of things she's good at.

Don't write, 'being a dodohead'.

Oh. Really? Damn.

JESS!

I'm joking!

6. Being an It Girl. The kind you look up to.

Seriously?! You think that?!

Yeah. I've always thought that. Even before your dad got engaged.

I wasn't expecting you to put something nice!!!

Me neither. I caved at the last moment.

Thanks.

You're welcome. Can we stop writing lists now?

Sure, we've finished this one.

Want to go play an epic prank on your dad?

I REALLY do.

Cool. I think Danny knows a guy who has some pet goats.

That sounds like an excellent start.

We're going to need more help, I reckon, if we want to make it really good.

I couldn't agree more.

We're going to need a strong team, captain.

You know what Jess? I think I might know where we can find one.

Acknowledgments

Big shout out to Lindsey Heaven, Jo Hayes, Alice Hill and the fantastic teams at Egmont and Bell Lomax Moreton. Thanks to you, Anna's adventures continue and I am forever grateful.

Huge thanks to all my friends. You guys have no idea just how genius you all are. Thank you for your incredible support and for inspiring me in all your brilliant, unique ways.

Special thanks to my amazing family. You're the best.

Finally, they say dogs are man's best friend. Amber, thanks for always being happy to see me, for keeping all my secrets and for growing up by my side. You have been this girl's best friend.

COMPETITION

We've teamed up with our lovely friends at
WE LOVE POP MAG to give **TEN LUCKY READERS**
the chance to **WIN** an amazing *It Girl* goody bag!
And if that wasn't enough, one lucky reader will also
WIN £250 worth of **TOPSHOP VOUCHERS**
to complete their perfect *It Girl* outfit! Just log into

www.welovepopmag.co.uk/win

to find out more!

GOOD LUCK!

Competition closes on 30th April 2016

WE ♥ POP.

CELEBRITIES BEFORE THEY WERE FAMOUS!

(Well, Anna anyway)

A special extract from the very first book in the brilliantly hilarious *the iT girl* series.

KATY BIRCHALL

the iTgirl

Everyone wants to be famous.

Don't they?

From: jess.delby@zingmail.co.uk
To: anna_huntley@zingmail.co.uk
Subject: Are you a pyromaniac?!

So I tried looking for you after school but someone said you'd gone home early. And I've been trying to call and you're not picking up your home phone or mobile, which I assume means you and Dog are watching something?

What happened today?? Is it true that you set the science block on fire??

Write back asap.

J x

From: anna_huntley@zingmail.co.uk
To: jess.delby@zingmail.co.uk
Subject: Re: Are you a pyromaniac?!

Dad's out on a date so Dog and I are passing the time by YouTube-ing scenes from *The Lion King*. The reason I can't pick up the phone is because I attempted to lift Dog up as though he was Simba on Pride Rock during that 'Circle of Life' song. Anyway, I couldn't do it and he fell back on to me, landing on my arm which now really hurts and I think I twisted my ankle so I'm staying put on the sofa.

I think he's put on a few pounds.

No, I didn't set the science block on fire. I set Josie Graham's hair on fire.

Love, me xxx

From: jess.delby@zingmail.co.uk
To: anna_huntley@zingmail.co.uk
Subject: ARE YOU INSANE?!

Why would you set fire to Ms Deputy Queen Bee's hair? You do realise that her mum once met Kate Moss? The school is really going to hate you, you know.

Is this because no one has asked you to the dance yet? Like

some kind of protest thing against all the girls who have been asked? It's not until the end of term – you've still got ages for someone to ask you.

J x

PS Why would you even think it was a good idea to try to lift a fully grown Labrador? Stop trying to act out movies, you weirdo.

From: anna_huntley@zingmail.co.uk
To: jess.delby@zingmail.co.uk
Subject: Re: ARE YOU INSANE?!

No, I am not insane. I just need to check that hairspray-laden girls aren't anywhere near Bunsen burners when I turn them on in the future.

The school definitely hates me. Josie looked like she was going to strangle me or something. I feared for my life. It was like that time I peed myself a little bit when the really scary IT teacher at my last school yelled at me for taking paper out of the printer.

Do you think she'll tell Sophie? Do you think Sophie will

hate me?

That would really be bad news because the other day I could have sworn that Sophie laughed at one of my jokes she overheard me telling Danny in the corridor. I thought that maybe she might not think I was such a loser after all.

And, excuse me, but I don't even *care* that no one's asked me to the dance. I don't need a date. Last time I went to a dance I didn't have a date and I was totally fine. I just danced with a balloon. It made everyone laugh but in a 'she's really funny' way not in a 'laughing at me' way.

Love, me xxx

From: jess.delby@zingmail.co.uk
To: anna_huntley@zingmail.co.uk
Subject: Um . . . I'm sorry . . . what?

That email was disturbing on so many levels.

You peed yourself? Dude, how old were you when this happened?

What do you mean you danced with a balloon?

You're making me nervous with all these weird stories from your past.

J x

From: anna_huntley@zingmail.co.uk
To: jess.delby@zingmail.co.uk
Subject: Re: Um . . . I'm sorry . . . what?

It was two years ago. But only a little pee. It wasn't like I wet myself. She just came out of nowhere and it gave me a fright.

Dancing with a balloon is a reasonable and funny thing to do. It's what Oscar Wilde would have done. It's a scathing comment on our society of dependent and irrational figures who consider themselves incomplete without a significant other.

Love, me xxx

From: jess.delby@zingmail.co.uk
To: anna_huntley@zingmail.co.uk
Subject: It is confirmed, you actually are insane

Maybe don't ever tell anyone else about that pee story.

Ditto the balloon one.

J x